JUST BEYOND™

VOLUME 3: A MONSTER'S LUNCH

Written by
R.L. Stine

Illustrated by
Kelly & Nichole Matthews

Lettered by
Mike Fiorentino

Cover by
Miguel Mercado

Just Beyond created by
R.L. Stine

Designer
Scott Newman

Assistant Editor
Michael Moccio

Editors
Whitney Leopard & Bryce Carlson

ABDOBOOKS.COM

Reinforced library bound edition published in 2021 by Spotlight, a division of ABDO, PO Box 398166, Minneapolis, Minnesota 55439. Spotlight produces high-quality reinforced library bound editions for schools and libraries. Published by agreement with KaBOOM!

Printed in the United States of America, North Mankato, Minnesota.
042020 092020

kaboom!™

JUST BEYOND: THE SCARE SCHOOL, September 2021. Published by KaBOOM!, a division of Boom Entertainment, Inc.

BOOM! Studios, 5670 Wilshire Boulevard, Suite 400, Los Angeles, CA 90036-5679.

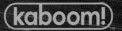

Library of Congress Control Number: 2019955592

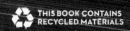

THIS BOOK CONTAINS RECYCLED MATERIALS

Publisher's Cataloging-in-Publication Data

Names: Stine, R.L., author. | Matthews, Kelly; Matthews, Nichole, illustrators.
Title: A monster's lunch / by R.L. Stine; illustrated by Kelly Matthews, and Nichole Matthews.
Description: Minneapolis, Minnesota: Spotlight, 2021. | Series: Just beyond; volume 3
Summary: Jess, Josh, and Marco follow a strange creature through a portal to a different realm where they end up at a school of horrors and are hunted by droggs.
Identifiers: ISBN 9781532144912 (lib. bdg.)
Subjects: LCSH: Middle school students--Juvenile fiction. | School buildings--Juvenile fiction. | Monsters--Juvenile fiction. | Supernatural--Juvenile fiction. | Fear--Juvenile fiction. | Graphic novels--Juvenile fiction.
Classification: DDC 741.5--dc23

A Division of ABDO
abdobooks.com

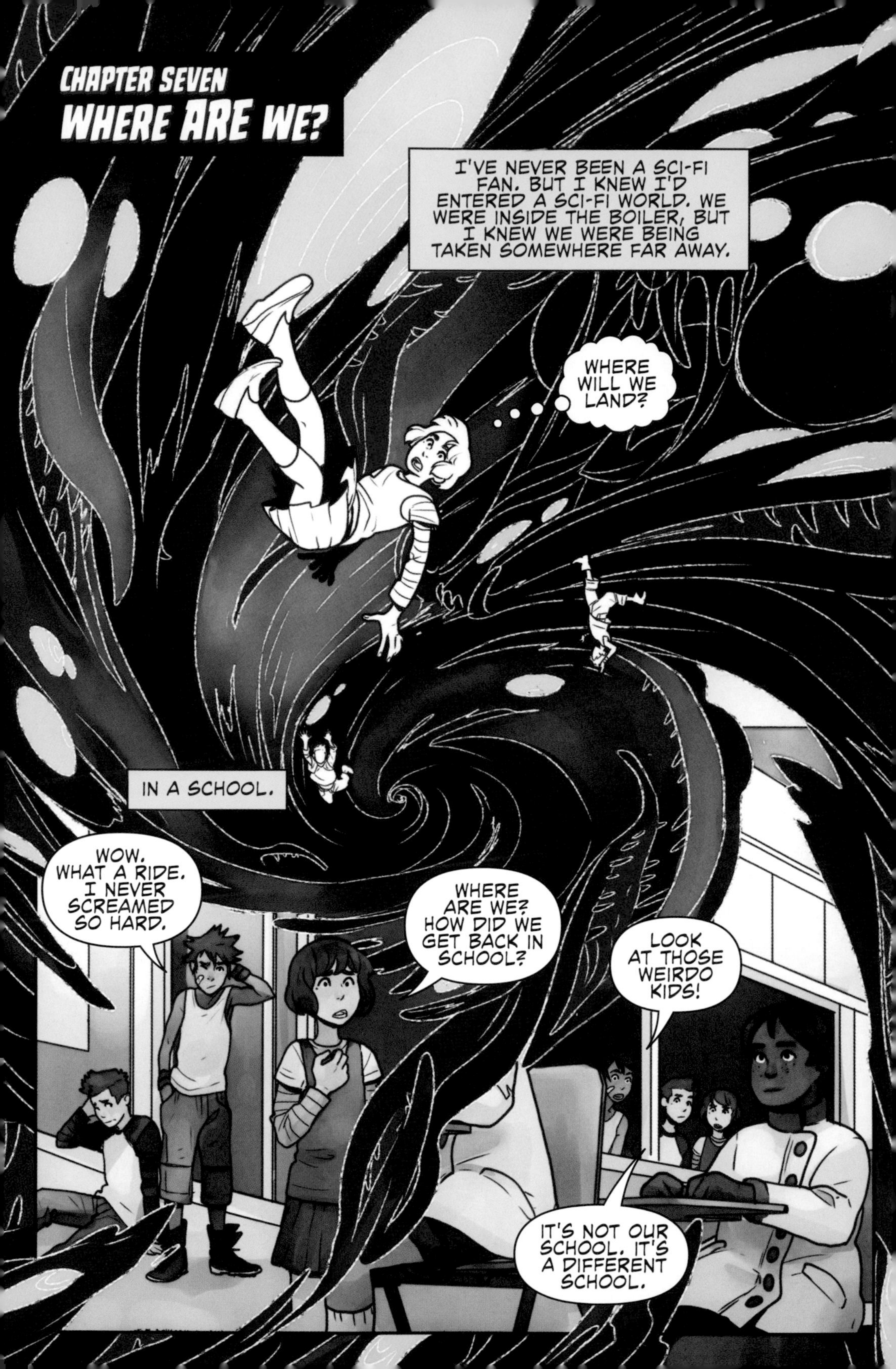
CHAPTER SEVEN
WHERE ARE WE?
I'VE NEVER BEEN A SCI-FI FAN. BUT I KNEW I'D ENTERED A SCI-FI WORLD. WE WERE INSIDE THE BOILER, BUT I KNEW WE WERE BEING TAKEN SOMEWHERE FAR AWAY.
WHERE WILL WE LAND?
IN A SCHOOL.
WOW. WHAT A RIDE. I NEVER SCREAMED SO HARD.
WHERE ARE WE? HOW DID WE GET BACK IN SCHOOL?
LOOK AT THOSE WEIRDO KIDS!
IT'S NOT OUR SCHOOL. IT'S A DIFFERENT SCHOOL.

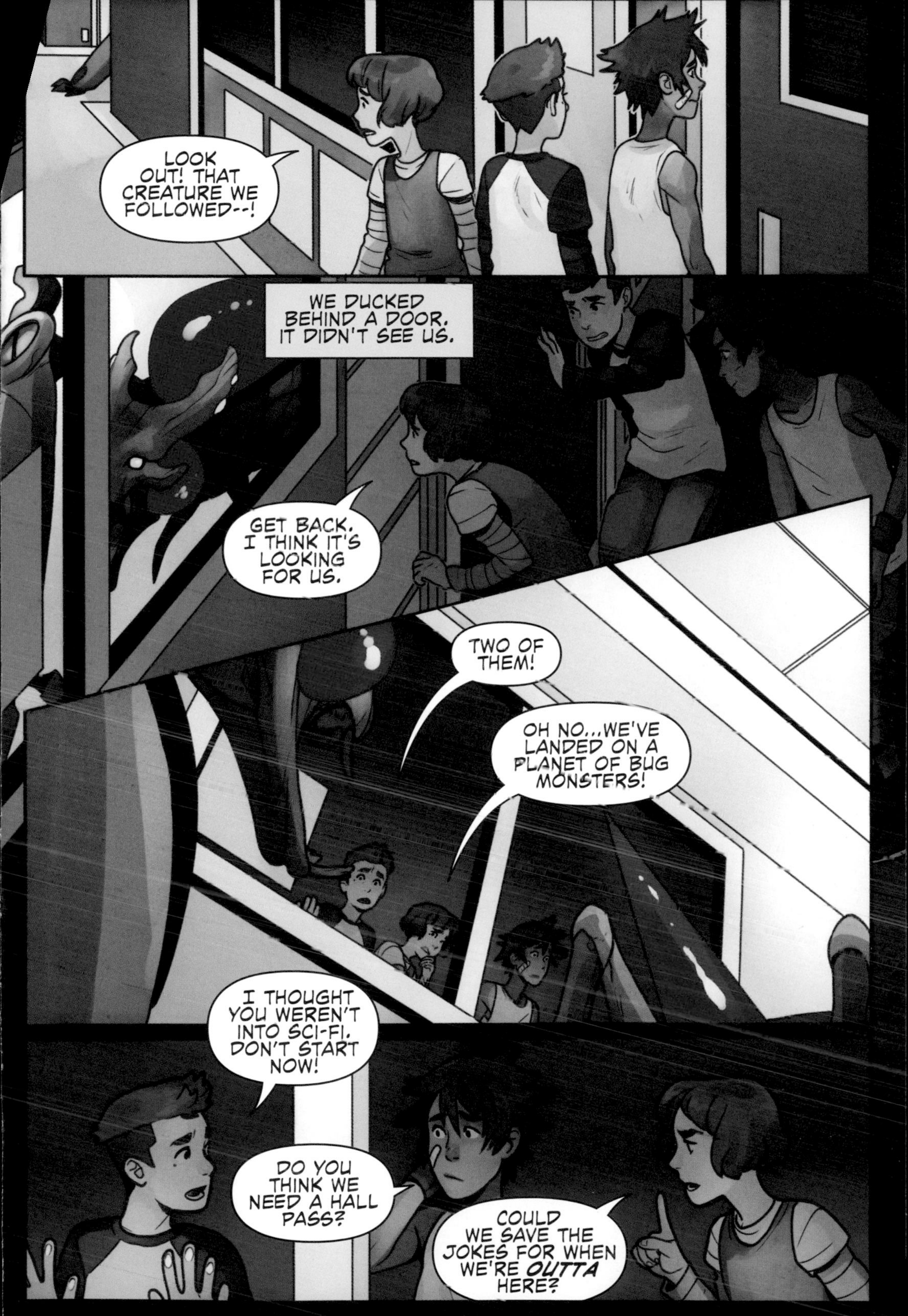
LOOK OUT! THAT CREATURE WE FOLLOWED--!
WE DUCKED BEHIND A DOOR. IT DIDN'T SEE US.
GET BACK. I THINK IT'S LOOKING FOR US.
TWO OF THEM!
OH NO...WE'VE LANDED ON A PLANET OF BUG MONSTERS!
I THOUGHT YOU WEREN'T INTO SCI-FI. DON'T START NOW!
DO YOU THINK WE NEED A HALL PASS?
COULD WE SAVE THE JOKES FOR WHEN WE'RE *OUTTA* HERE?

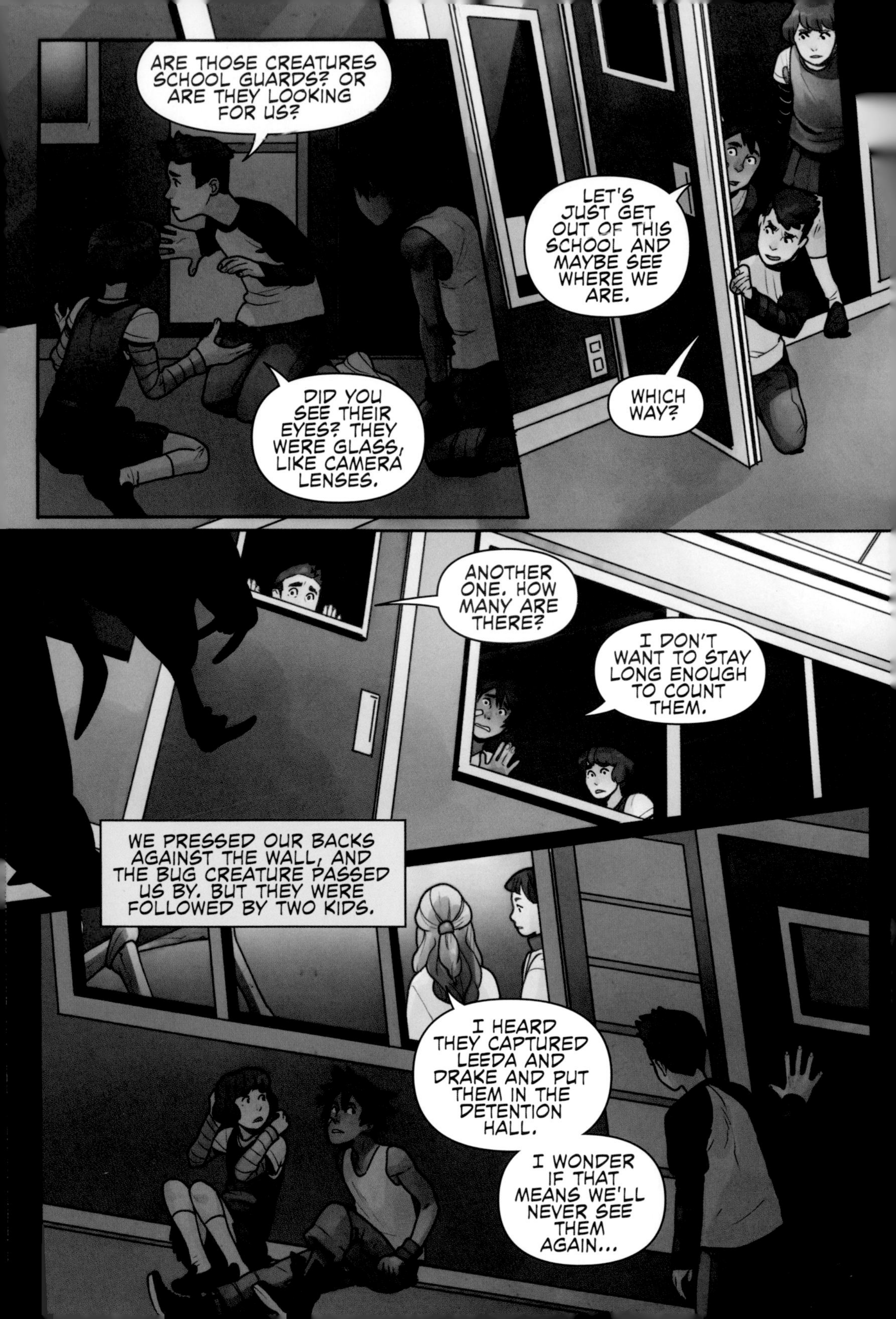
ARE THOSE CREATURES SCHOOL GUARDS? OR ARE THEY LOOKING FOR US?
LET'S JUST GET OUT OF THIS SCHOOL AND MAYBE SEE WHERE WE ARE.
DID YOU SEE THEIR EYES? THEY WERE GLASS, LIKE CAMERA LENSES.
WHICH WAY?
ANOTHER ONE. HOW MANY ARE THERE?
I DON'T WANT TO STAY LONG ENOUGH TO COUNT THEM.
WE PRESSED OUR BACKS AGAINST THE WALL, AND THE BUG CREATURE PASSED US BY. BUT THEY WERE FOLLOWED BY TWO KIDS.
I HEARD THEY CAPTURED LEEDA AND DRAKE AND PUT THEM IN THE DETENTION HALL.
I WONDER IF THAT MEANS WE'LL NEVER SEE THEM AGAIN...

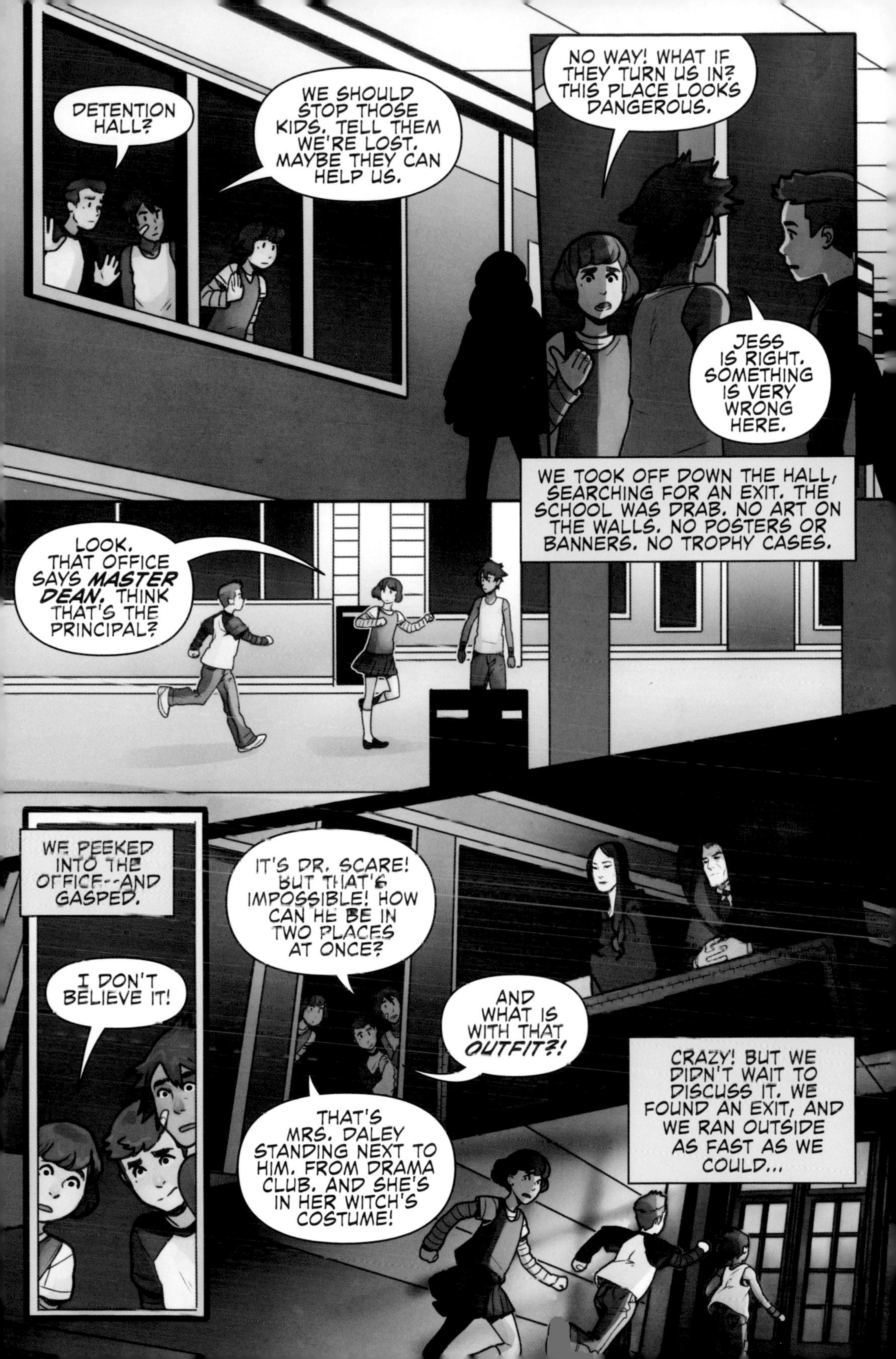
DETENTION HALL?
WE SHOULD STOP THOSE KIDS. TELL THEM WE'RE LOST. MAYBE THEY CAN HELP US.
NO WAY! WHAT IF THEY TURN US IN? THIS PLACE LOOKS DANGEROUS.
JESS IS RIGHT. SOMETHING IS VERY WRONG HERE.
WE TOOK OFF DOWN THE HALL, SEARCHING FOR AN EXIT. THE SCHOOL WAS DRAB. NO ART ON THE WALLS. NO POSTERS OR BANNERS. NO TROPHY CASES.
LOOK. THAT OFFICE SAYS *MASTER DEAN.* THINK THAT'S THE PRINCIPAL?
WE PEEKED INTO THE OFFICE--AND GASPED.
I DON'T BELIEVE IT!
IT'S DR. SCARE! BUT THAT'S IMPOSSIBLE! HOW CAN HE BE IN TWO PLACES AT ONCE?
THAT'S MRS. DALEY STANDING NEXT TO HIM. FROM DRAMA CLUB. AND SHE'S IN HER WITCH'S COSTUME!
AND WHAT IS WITH THAT *OUTFIT?!*
CRAZY! BUT WE DIDN'T WAIT TO DISCUSS IT. WE FOUND AN EXIT, AND WE RAN OUTSIDE AS FAST AS WE COULD...

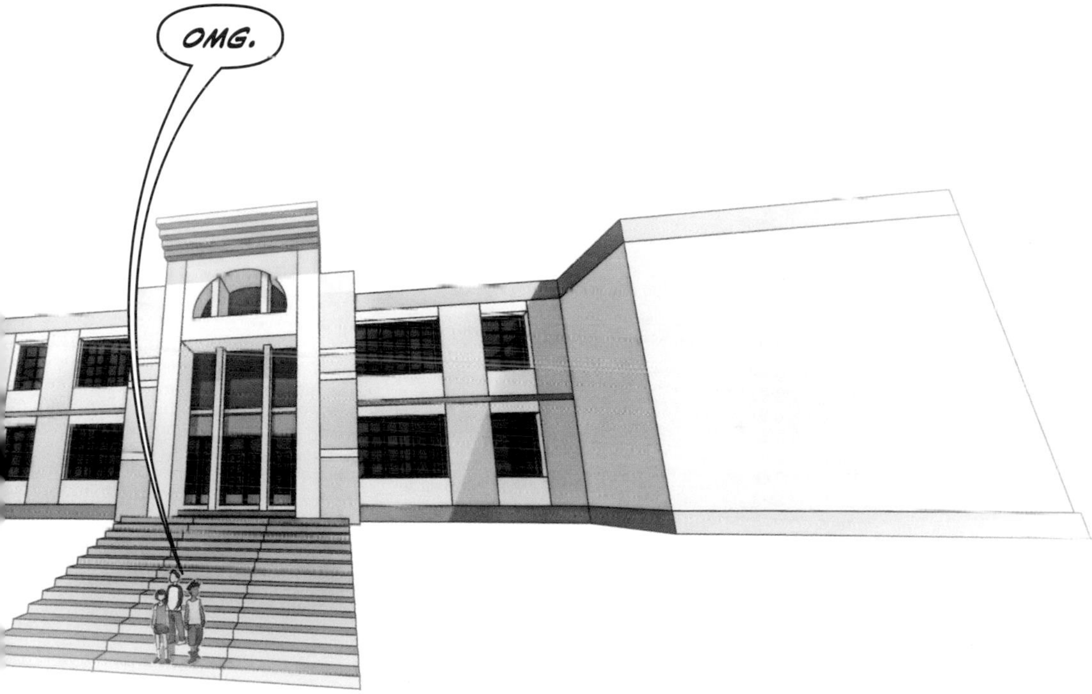
OMG.

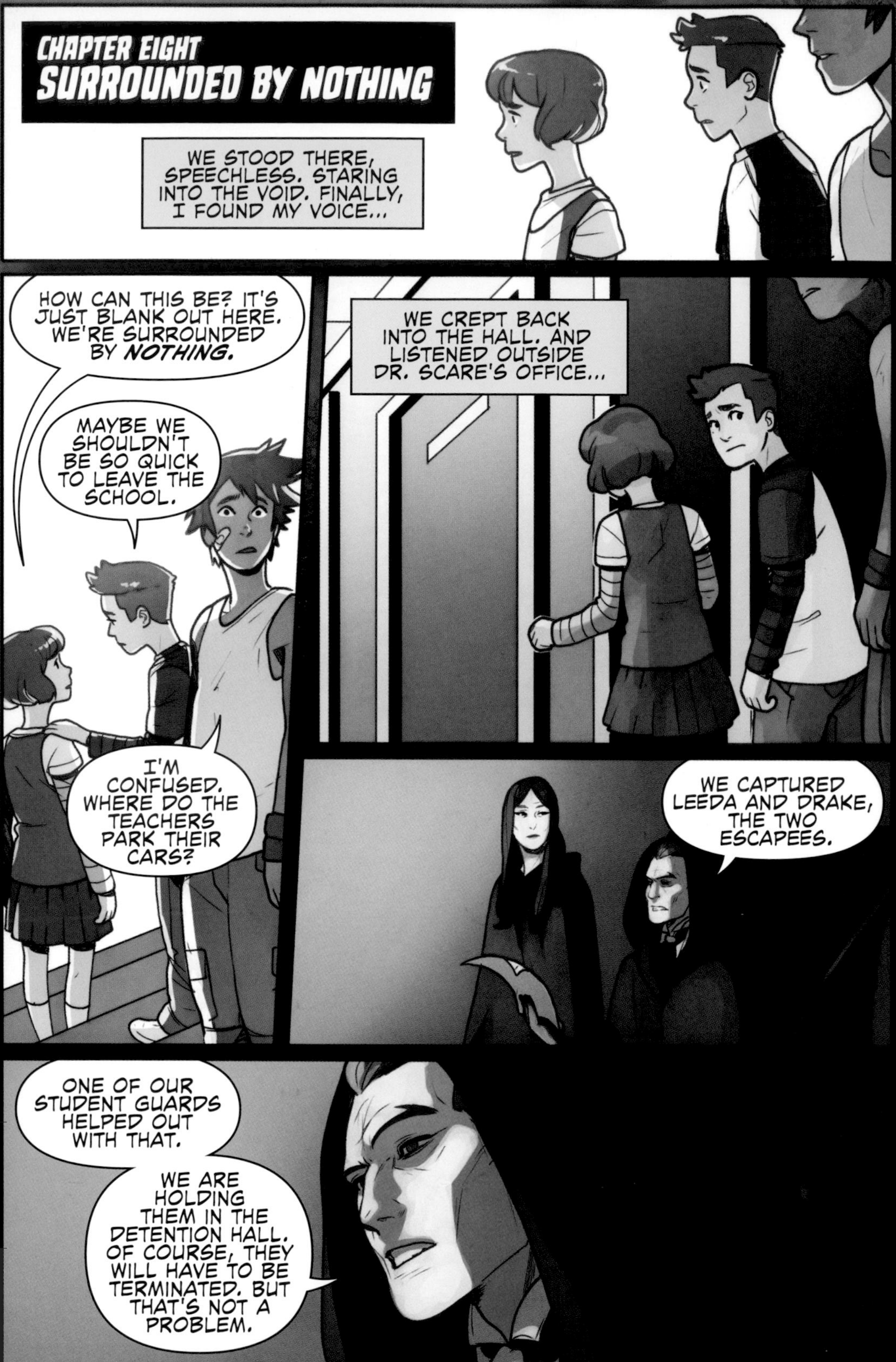
CHAPTER EIGHT
SURROUNDED BY NOTHING
WE STOOD THERE, SPEECHLESS. STARING INTO THE VOID. FINALLY, I FOUND MY VOICE...
HOW CAN THIS BE? IT'S JUST BLANK OUT HERE. WE'RE SURROUNDED BY NOTHING.
MAYBE WE SHOULDN'T BE SO QUICK TO LEAVE THE SCHOOL.
I'M CONFUSED. WHERE DO THE TEACHERS PARK THEIR CARS?
WE CREPT BACK INTO THE HALL. AND LISTENED OUTSIDE DR. SCARE'S OFFICE...
WE CAPTURED LEEDA AND DRAKE, THE TWO ESCAPEES.
ONE OF OUR STUDENT GUARDS HELPED OUT WITH THAT.
WE ARE HOLDING THEM IN THE DETENTION HALL. OF COURSE, THEY WILL HAVE TO BE TERMINATED. BUT THAT'S NOT A PROBLEM.

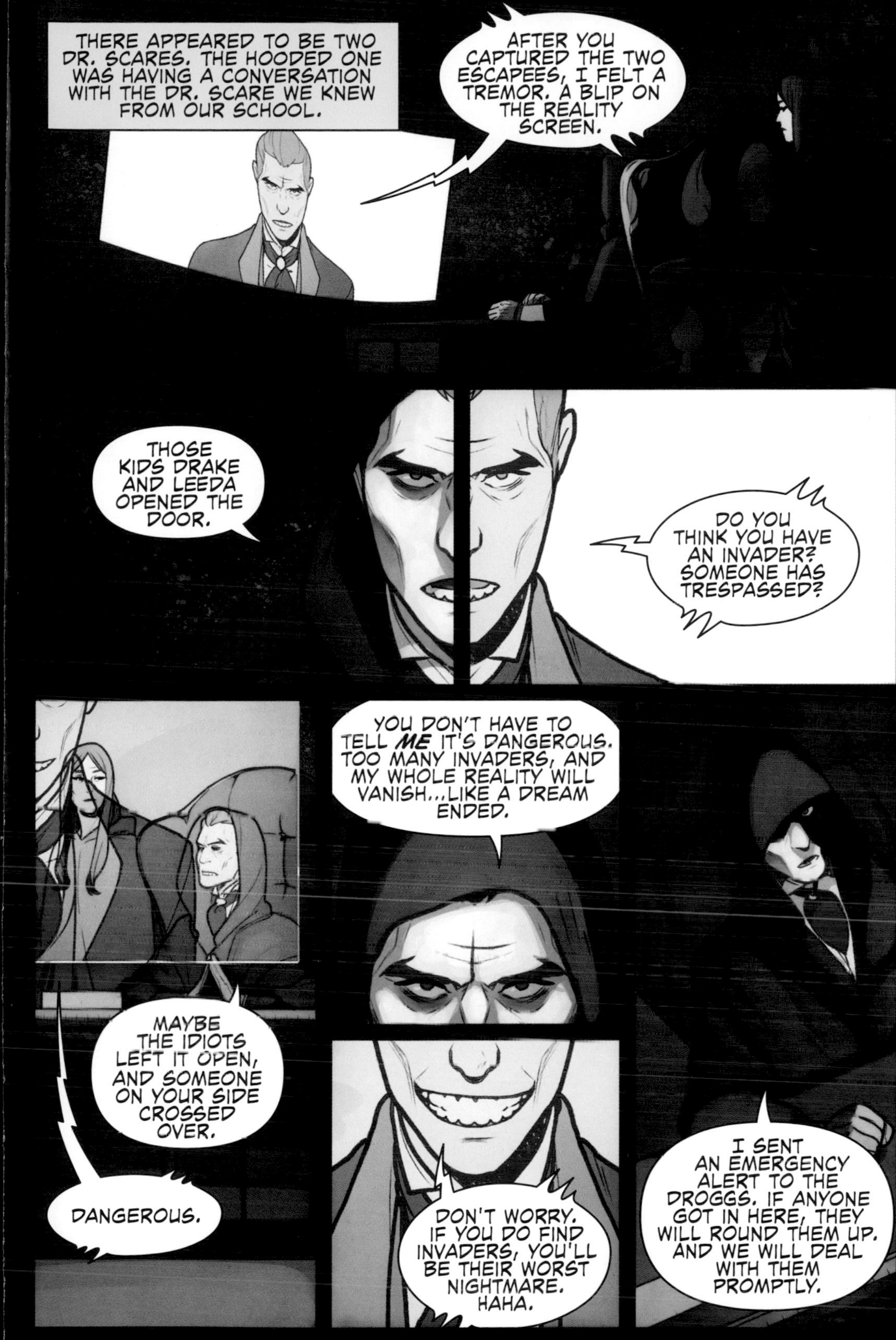
THERE APPEARED TO BE TWO DR. SCARES. THE HOODED ONE WAS HAVING A CONVERSATION WITH THE DR. SCARE WE KNEW FROM OUR SCHOOL.
AFTER YOU CAPTURED THE TWO ESCAPEES, I FELT A TREMOR. A BLIP ON THE REALITY SCREEN.
THOSE KIDS DRAKE AND LEEDA OPENED THE DOOR.
DO YOU THINK YOU HAVE AN INVADER? SOMEONE HAS TRESPASSED?
YOU DON'T HAVE TO TELL *ME* IT'S DANGEROUS. TOO MANY INVADERS, AND MY WHOLE REALITY WILL VANISH...LIKE A DREAM ENDED.
MAYBE THE IDIOTS LEFT IT OPEN, AND SOMEONE ON YOUR SIDE CROSSED OVER.
DANGEROUS.
DON'T WORRY. IF YOU DO FIND INVADERS, YOU'LL BE THEIR WORST NIGHTMARE. HAHA.
I SENT AN EMERGENCY ALERT TO THE DROGGS. IF ANYONE GOT IN HERE, THEY WILL ROUND THEM UP. AND WE WILL DEAL WITH THEM PROMPTLY.

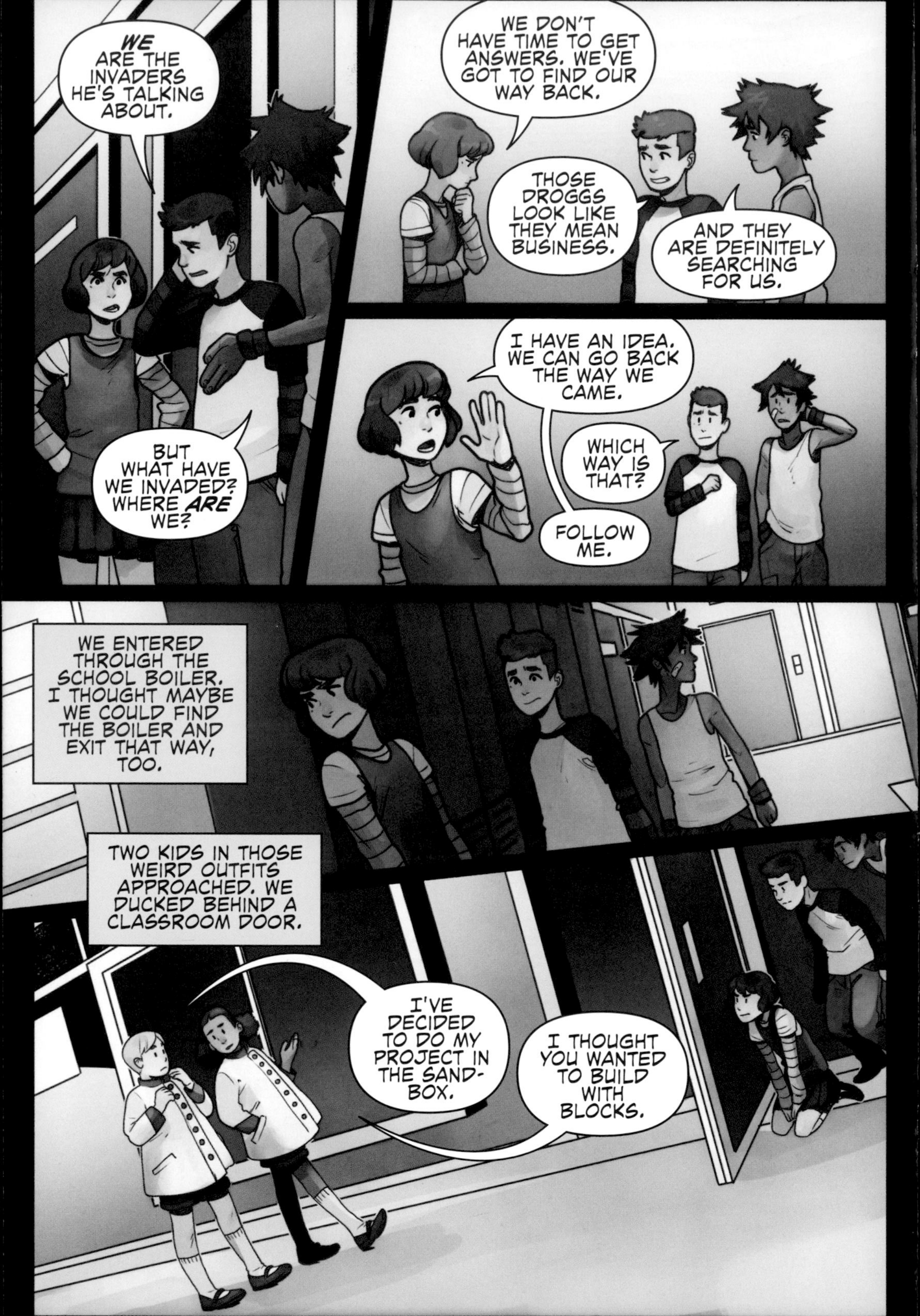
WE ARE THE INVADERS HE'S TALKING ABOUT.
BUT WHAT HAVE WE INVADED? WHERE ARE WE?
WE DON'T HAVE TIME TO GET ANSWERS. WE'VE GOT TO FIND OUR WAY BACK.
THOSE DROGGS LOOK LIKE THEY MEAN BUSINESS.
AND THEY ARE DEFINITELY SEARCHING FOR US.
I HAVE AN IDEA. WE CAN GO BACK THE WAY WE CAME.
WHICH WAY IS THAT?
FOLLOW ME.
WE ENTERED THROUGH THE SCHOOL BOILER. I THOUGHT MAYBE WE COULD FIND THE BOILER AND EXIT THAT WAY, TOO.
TWO KIDS IN THOSE WEIRD OUTFITS APPROACHED. WE DUCKED BEHIND A CLASSROOM DOOR.
I'VE DECIDED TO DO MY PROJECT IN THE SAND-BOX.
I THOUGHT YOU WANTED TO BUILD WITH BLOCKS.

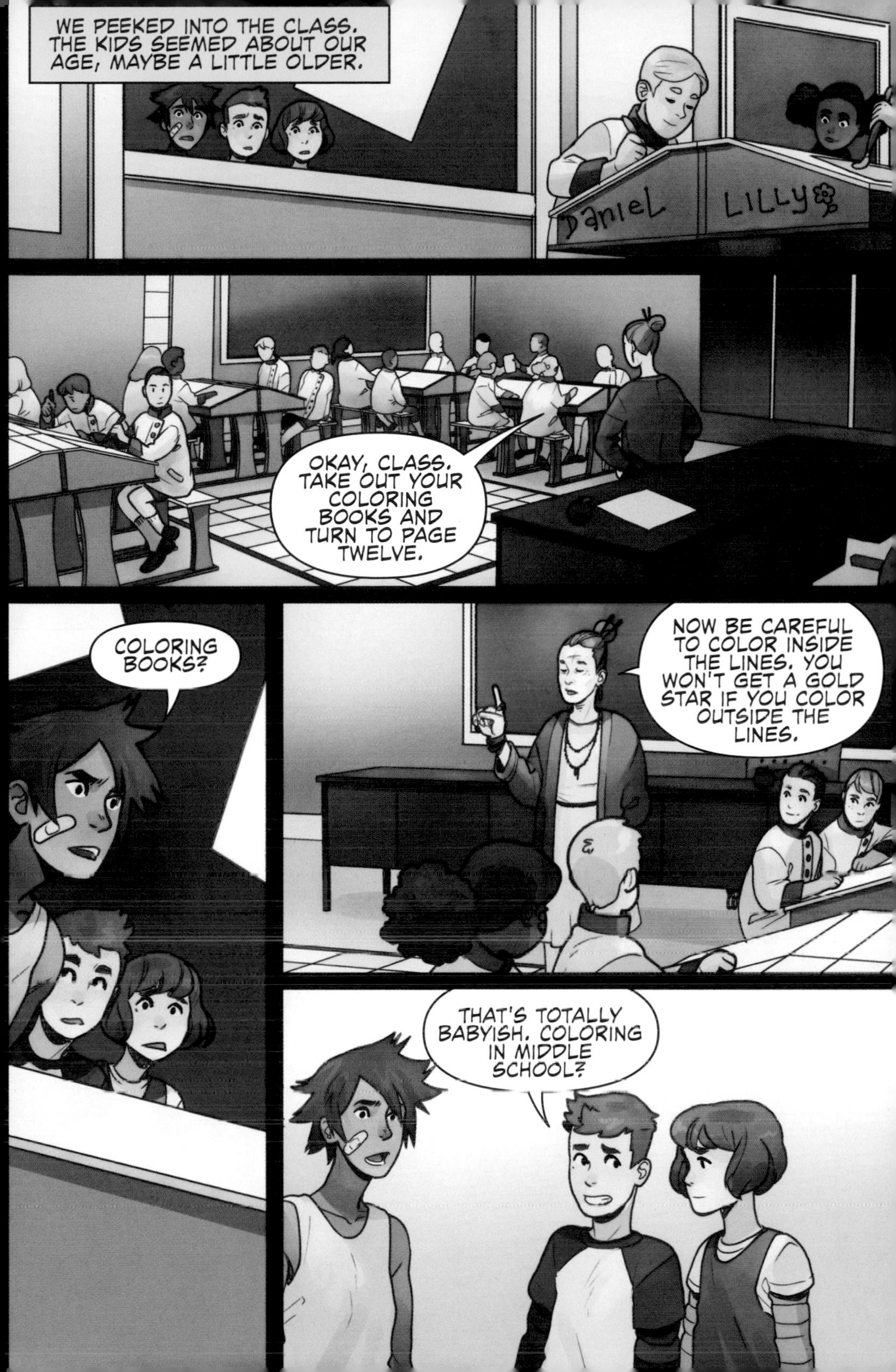
WE PEEKED INTO THE CLASS. THE KIDS SEEMED ABOUT OUR AGE, MAYBE A LITTLE OLDER.
DaNieL
LILLY
OKAY, CLASS. TAKE OUT YOUR COLORING BOOKS AND TURN TO PAGE TWELVE.
COLORING BOOKS?
NOW BE CAREFUL TO COLOR INSIDE THE LINES. YOU WON'T GET A GOLD STAR IF YOU COLOR OUTSIDE THE LINES.
THAT'S TOTALLY BABYISH. COLORING IN MIDDLE SCHOOL?

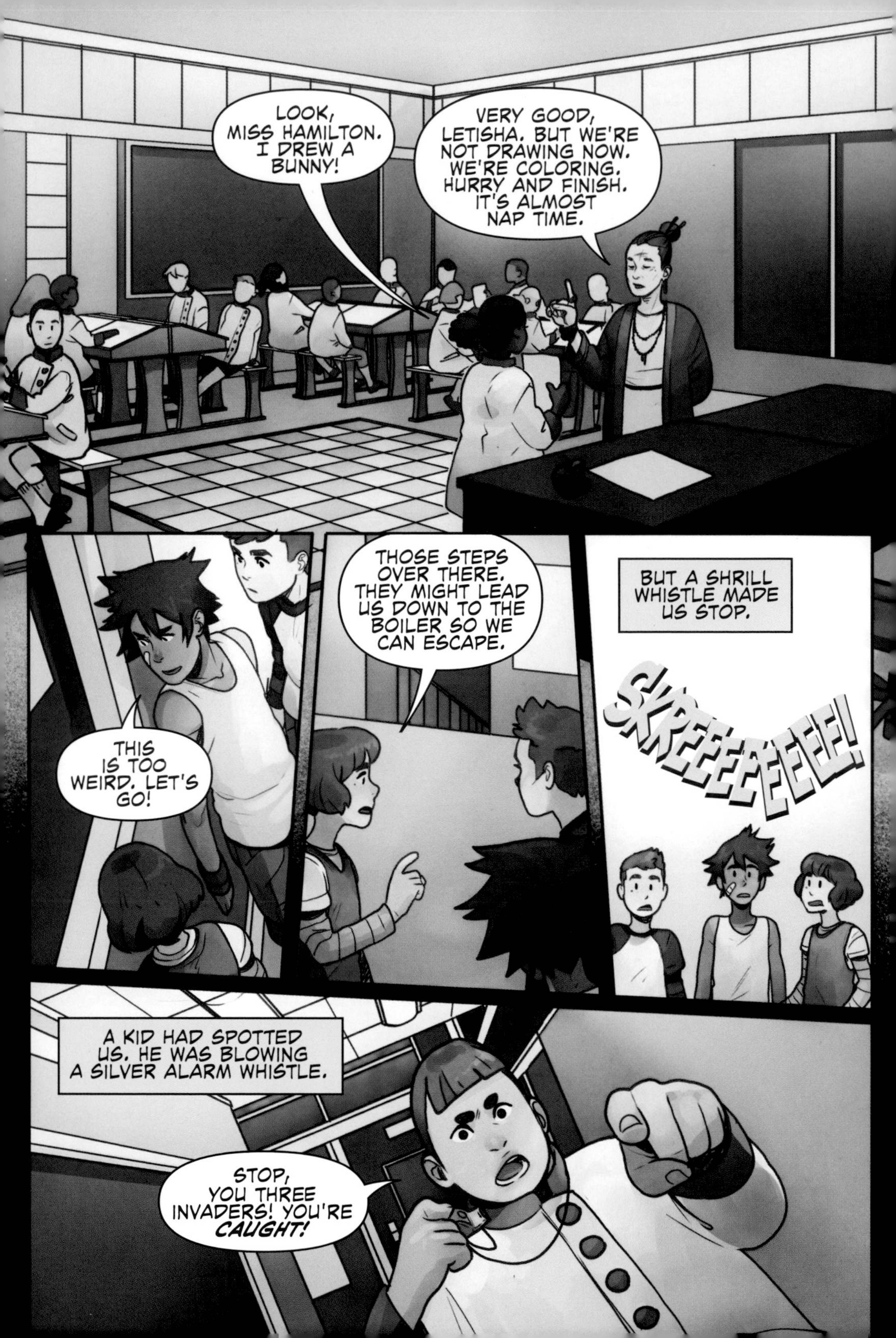
LOOK, MISS HAMILTON. I DREW A BUNNY!
VERY GOOD, LETISHA. BUT WE'RE NOT DRAWING NOW. WE'RE COLORING. HURRY AND FINISH. IT'S ALMOST NAP TIME.
THIS IS TOO WEIRD. LET'S GO!
THOSE STEPS OVER THERE. THEY MIGHT LEAD US DOWN TO THE BOILER SO WE CAN ESCAPE.
BUT A SHRILL WHISTLE MADE US STOP.
SKREEEEEEEEE!
A KID HAD SPOTTED US. HE WAS BLOWING A SILVER ALARM WHISTLE.
STOP, YOU THREE INVADERS! YOU'RE *CAUGHT!*

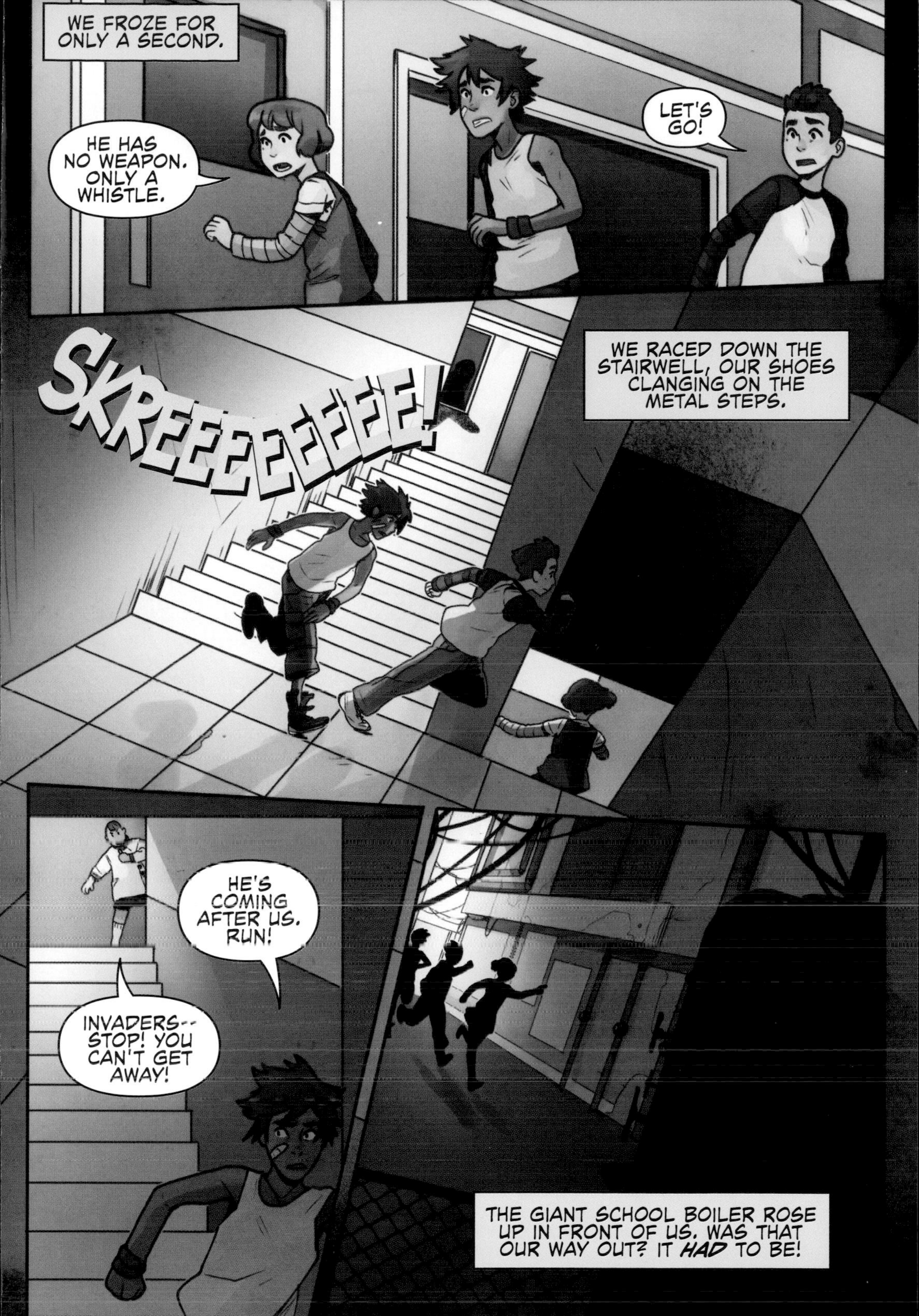
WE FROZE FOR ONLY A SECOND.
HE HAS NO WEAPON. ONLY A WHISTLE.
LET'S GO!
SKREEEEEEEEE!
WE RACED DOWN THE STAIRWELL, OUR SHOES CLANGING ON THE METAL STEPS.
HE'S COMING AFTER US. RUN!
INVADERS-- STOP! YOU CAN'T GET AWAY!
THE GIANT SCHOOL BOILER ROSE UP IN FRONT OF US. WAS THAT OUR WAY OUT? IT *HAD* TO BE!

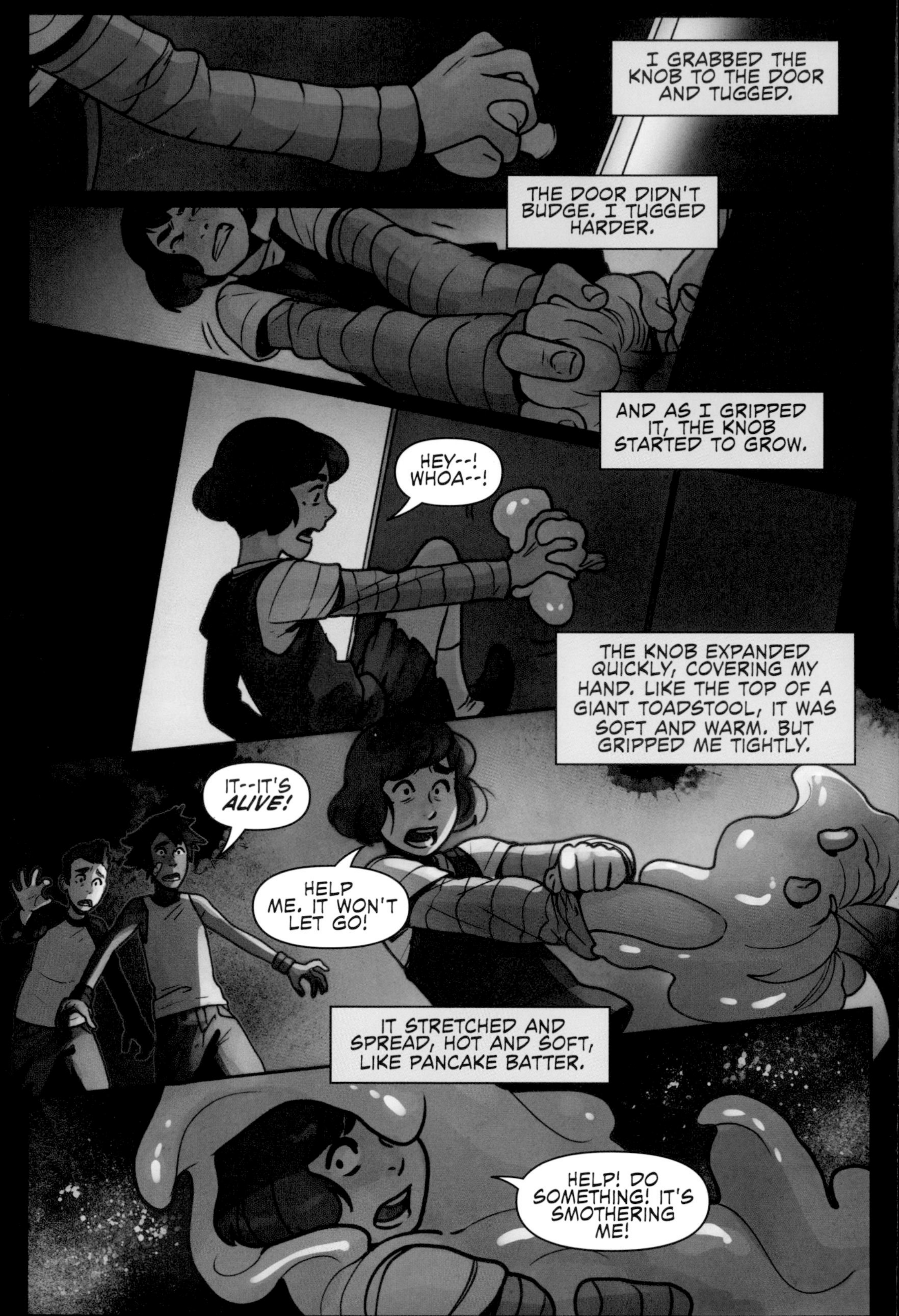
I GRABBED THE KNOB TO THE DOOR AND TUGGED.
THE DOOR DIDN'T BUDGE. I TUGGED HARDER.
AND AS I GRIPPED IT, THE KNOB STARTED TO GROW.
HEY--! WHOA--!
THE KNOB EXPANDED QUICKLY, COVERING MY HAND. LIKE THE TOP OF A GIANT TOADSTOOL, IT WAS SOFT AND WARM. BUT GRIPPED ME TIGHTLY.
IT--IT'S *ALIVE!*
HELP ME. IT WON'T LET GO!
IT STRETCHED AND SPREAD, HOT AND SOFT, LIKE PANCAKE BATTER.
HELP! DO SOMETHING! IT'S SMOTHERING ME!

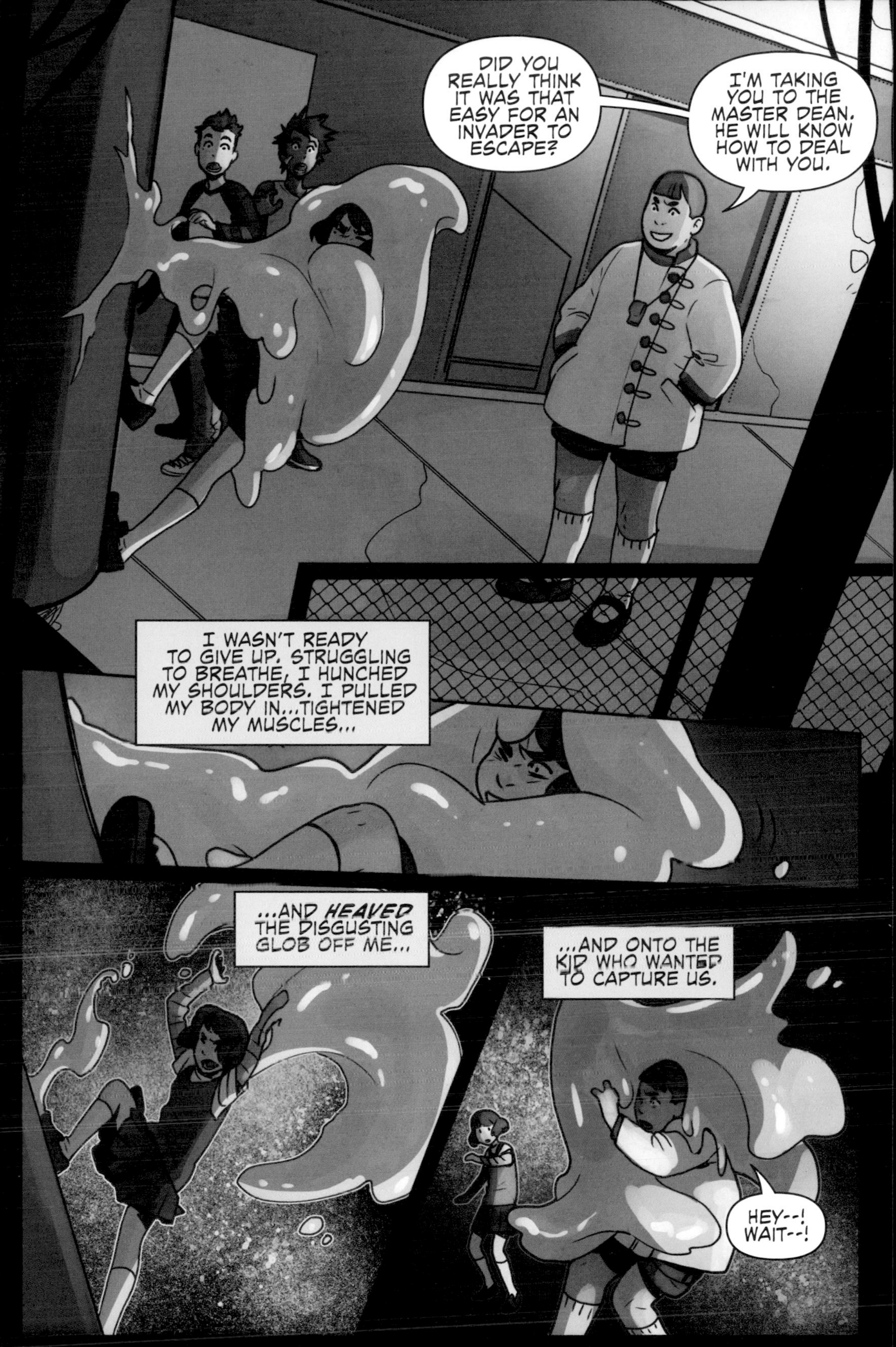
DID YOU REALLY THINK IT WAS THAT EASY FOR AN INVADER TO ESCAPE?
I'M TAKING YOU TO THE MASTER DEAN. HE WILL KNOW HOW TO DEAL WITH YOU.
I WASN'T READY TO GIVE UP. STRUGGLING TO BREATHE, I HUNCHED MY SHOULDERS. I PULLED MY BODY IN...TIGHTENED MY MUSCLES...
...AND *HEAVED* THE DISGUSTING GLOB OFF ME...
...AND ONTO THE KID WHO WANTED TO CAPTURE US.
HEY--! WAIT--!

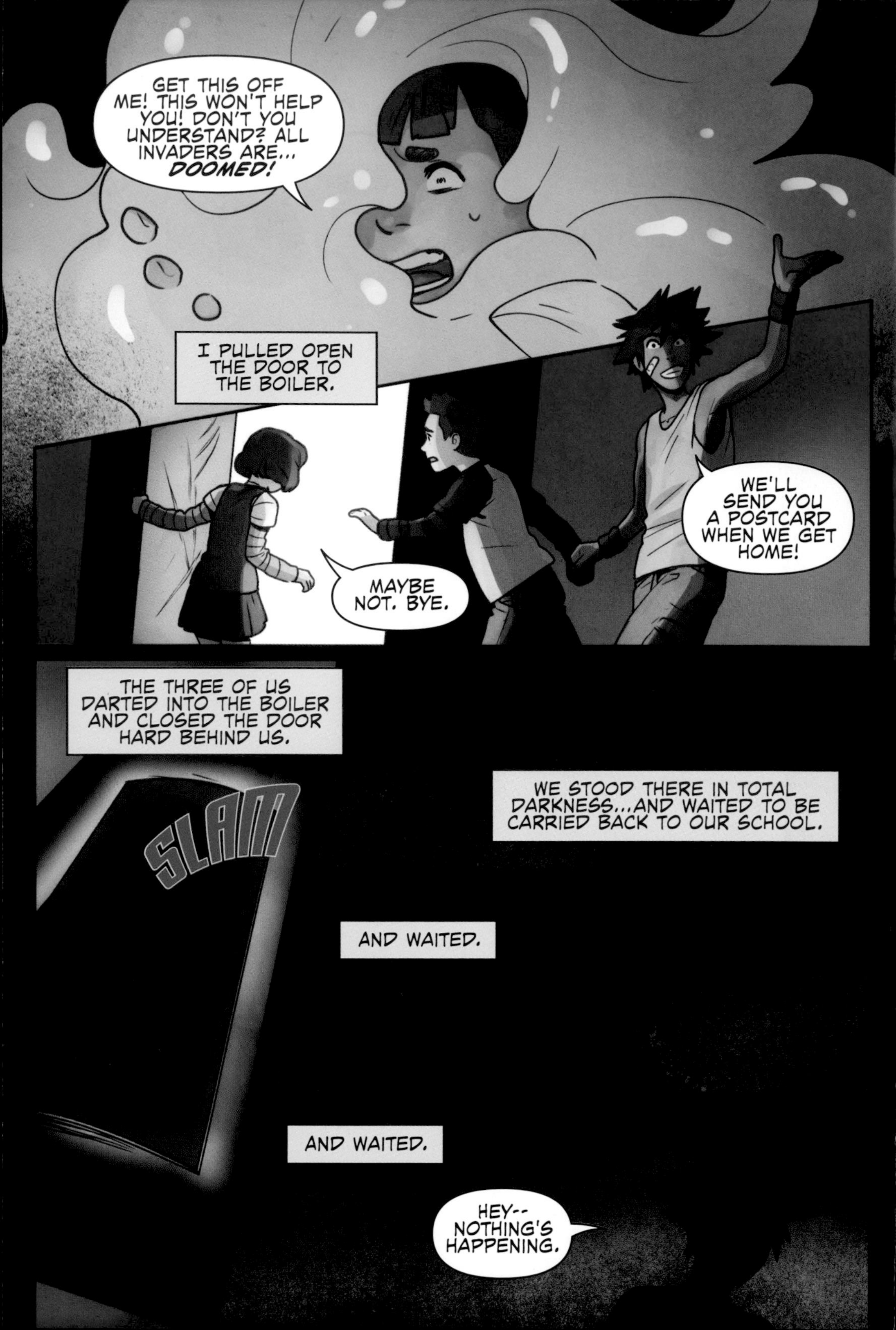
GET THIS OFF ME! THIS WON'T HELP YOU! DON'T YOU UNDERSTAND? ALL INVADERS ARE... DOOMED!
I PULLED OPEN THE DOOR TO THE BOILER.
WE'LL SEND YOU A POSTCARD WHEN WE GET HOME!
MAYBE NOT. BYE.
THE THREE OF US DARTED INTO THE BOILER AND CLOSED THE DOOR HARD BEHIND US.
SLAM
WE STOOD THERE IN TOTAL DARKNESS...AND WAITED TO BE CARRIED BACK TO OUR SCHOOL.
AND WAITED.
AND WAITED.
HEY-- NOTHING'S HAPPENING.

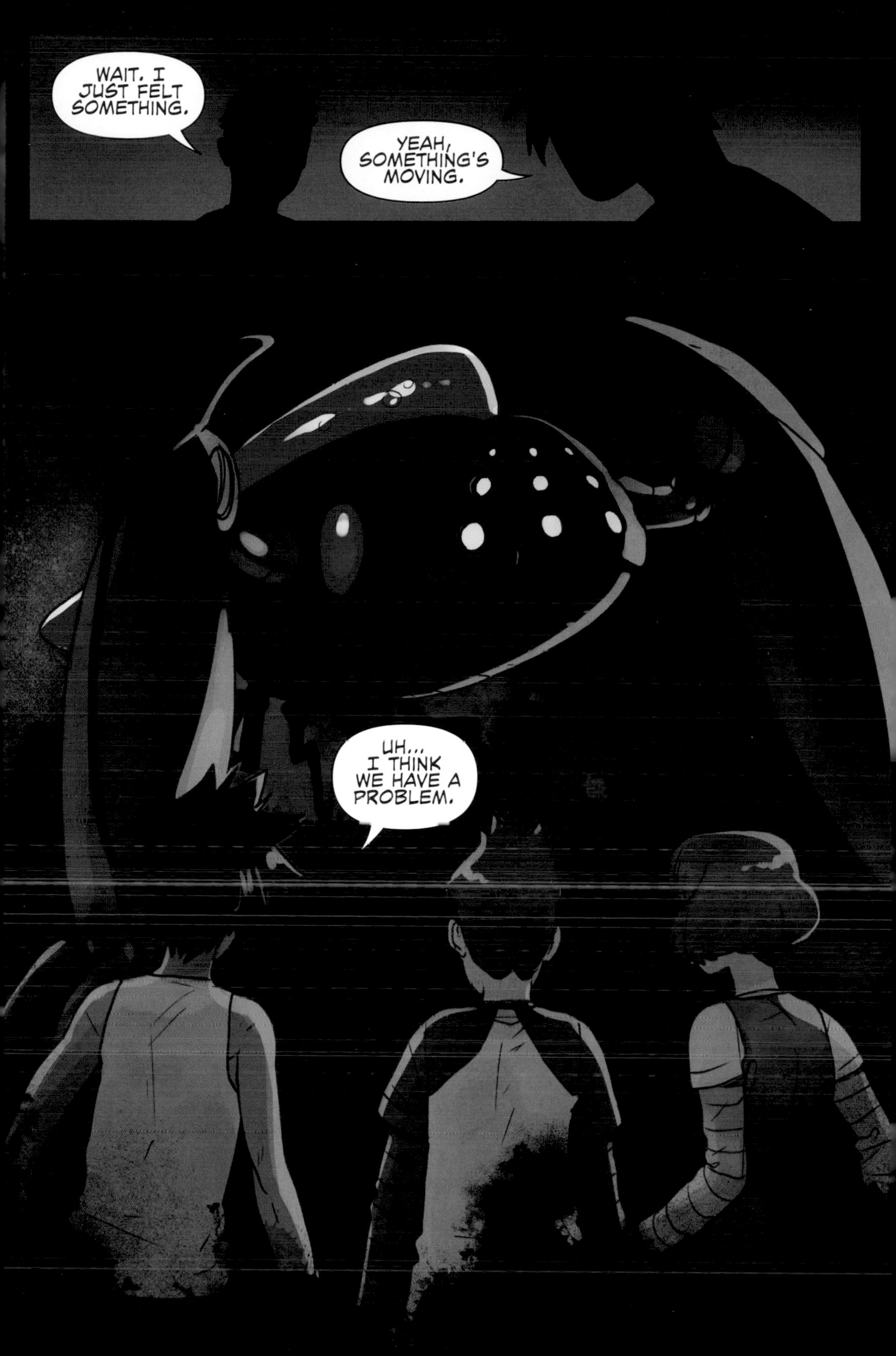
WAIT. I JUST FELT SOMETHING.
YEAH, SOMETHING'S MOVING.
UH... I THINK WE HAVE A PROBLEM.

CHAPTER NINE
A MONSTER'S LUNCH

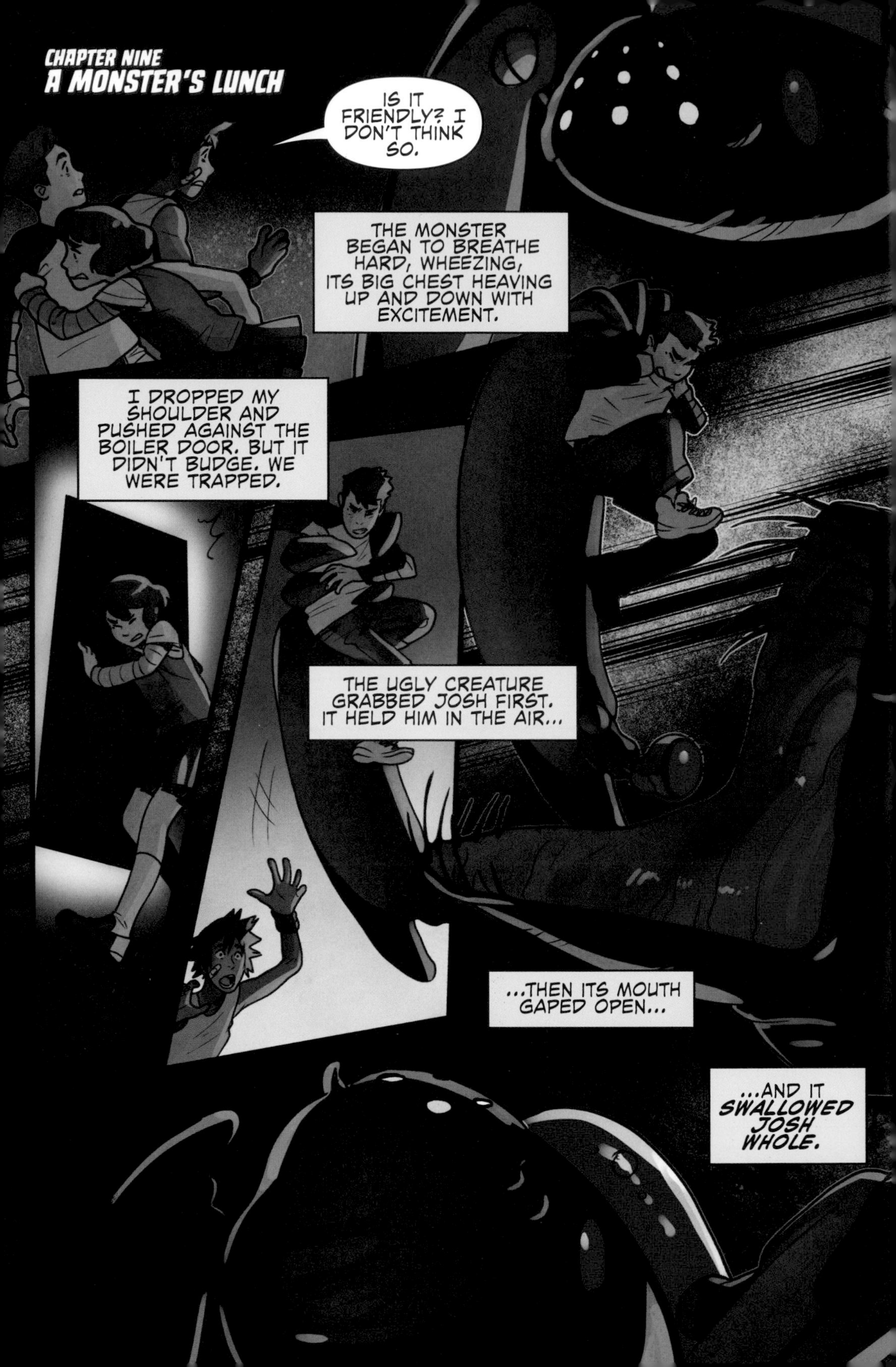
IS IT FRIENDLY? I DON'T THINK SO.
THE MONSTER BEGAN TO BREATHE HARD, WHEEZING, ITS BIG CHEST HEAVING UP AND DOWN WITH EXCITEMENT.
I DROPPED MY SHOULDER AND PUSHED AGAINST THE BOILER DOOR. BUT IT DIDN'T BUDGE. WE WERE TRAPPED.
THE UGLY CREATURE GRABBED JOSH FIRST. IT HELD HIM IN THE AIR...
...THEN ITS MOUTH GAPED OPEN...
...AND IT *SWALLOWED JOSH WHOLE.*

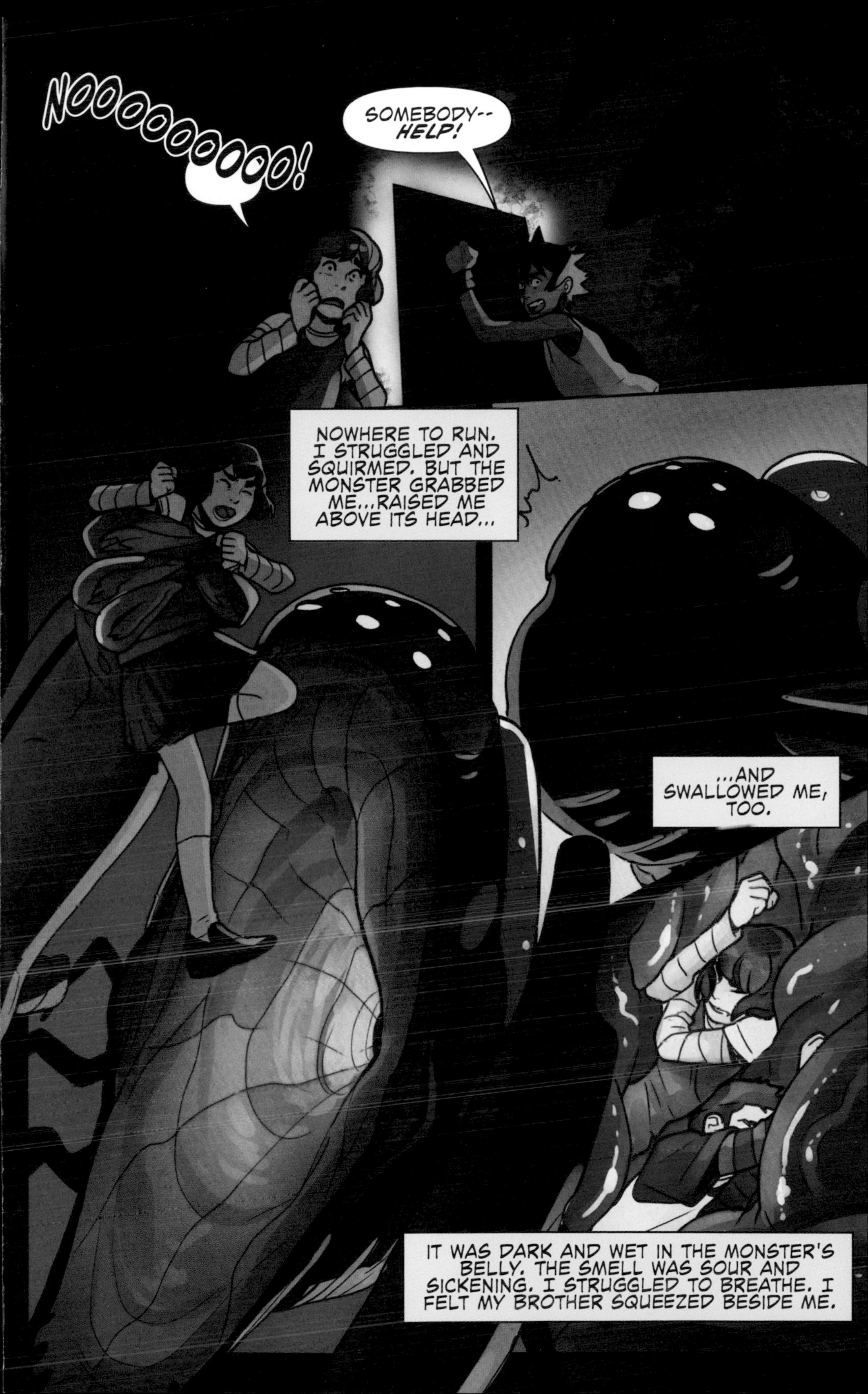
NOOOOOOOOOO!
SOMEBODY-- HELP!
NOWHERE TO RUN. I STRUGGLED AND SQUIRMED. BUT THE MONSTER GRABBED ME...RAISED ME ABOVE ITS HEAD...
...AND SWALLOWED ME, TOO.
IT WAS DARK AND WET IN THE MONSTER'S BELLY. THE SMELL WAS SOUR AND SICKENING. I STRUGGLED TO BREATHE. I FELT MY BROTHER SQUEEZED BESIDE ME.

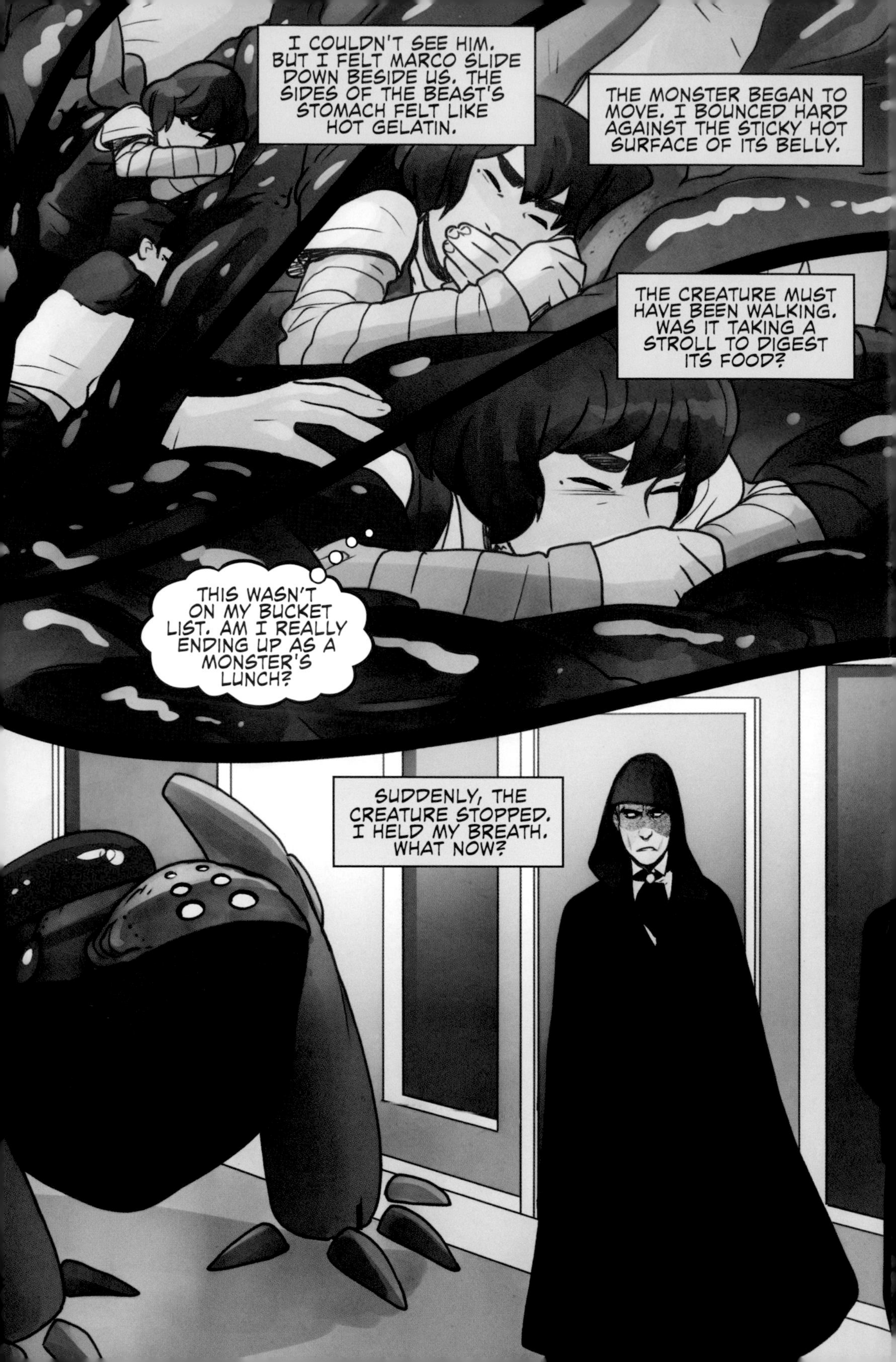
I COULDN'T SEE HIM. BUT I FELT MARCO SLIDE DOWN BESIDE US. THE SIDES OF THE BEAST'S STOMACH FELT LIKE HOT GELATIN.
THE MONSTER BEGAN TO MOVE. I BOUNCED HARD AGAINST THE STICKY HOT SURFACE OF ITS BELLY.
THE CREATURE MUST HAVE BEEN WALKING. WAS IT TAKING A STROLL TO DIGEST ITS FOOD?
THIS WASN'T ON MY BUCKET LIST. AM I REALLY ENDING UP AS A MONSTER'S LUNCH?
SUDDENLY, THE CREATURE STOPPED. I HELD MY BREATH. WHAT NOW?

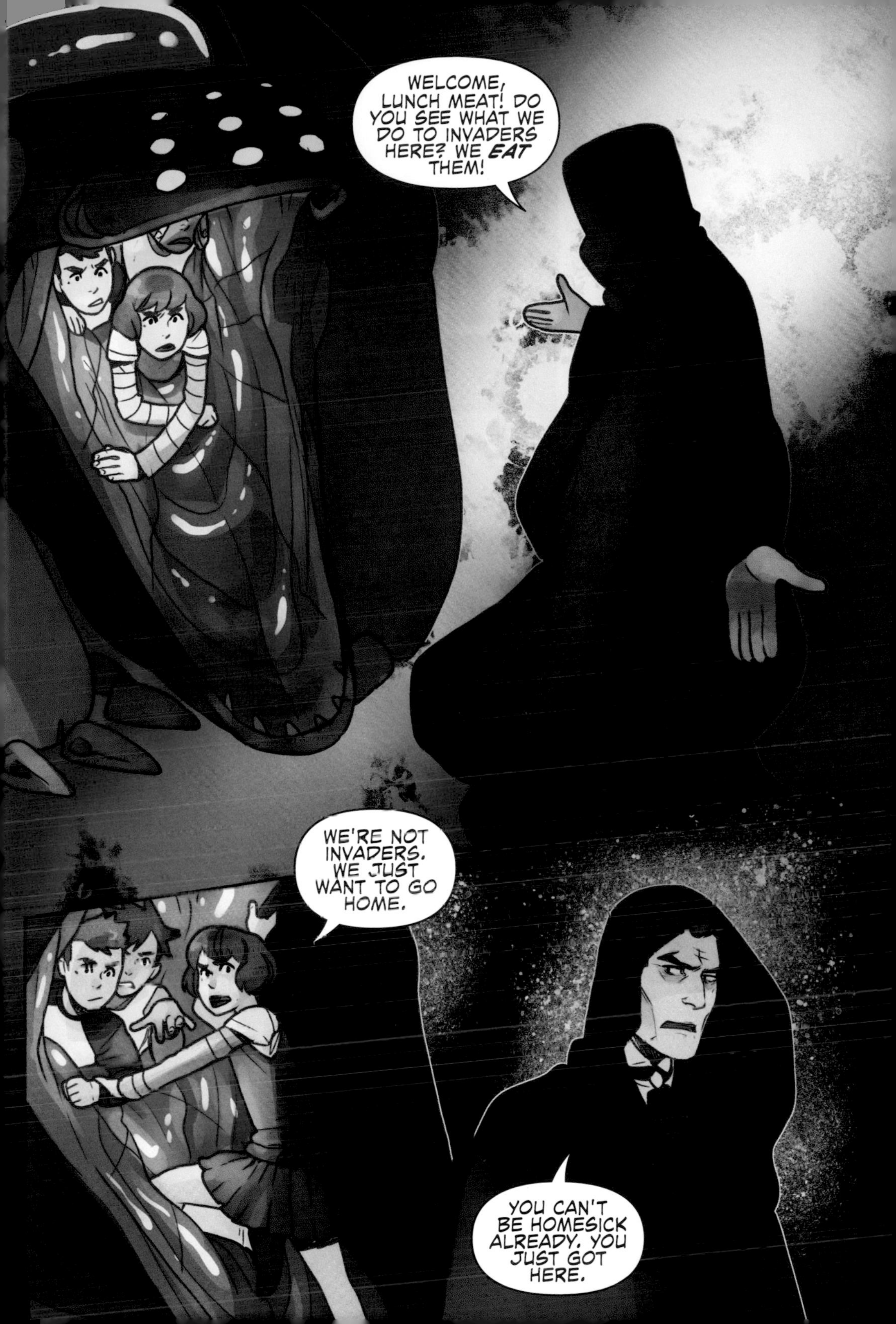
WELCOME, LUNCH MEAT! DO YOU SEE WHAT WE DO TO INVADERS HERE? WE *EAT* THEM!
WE'RE NOT INVADERS. WE JUST WANT TO GO HOME.
YOU CAN'T BE HOMESICK ALREADY. YOU JUST GOT HERE.

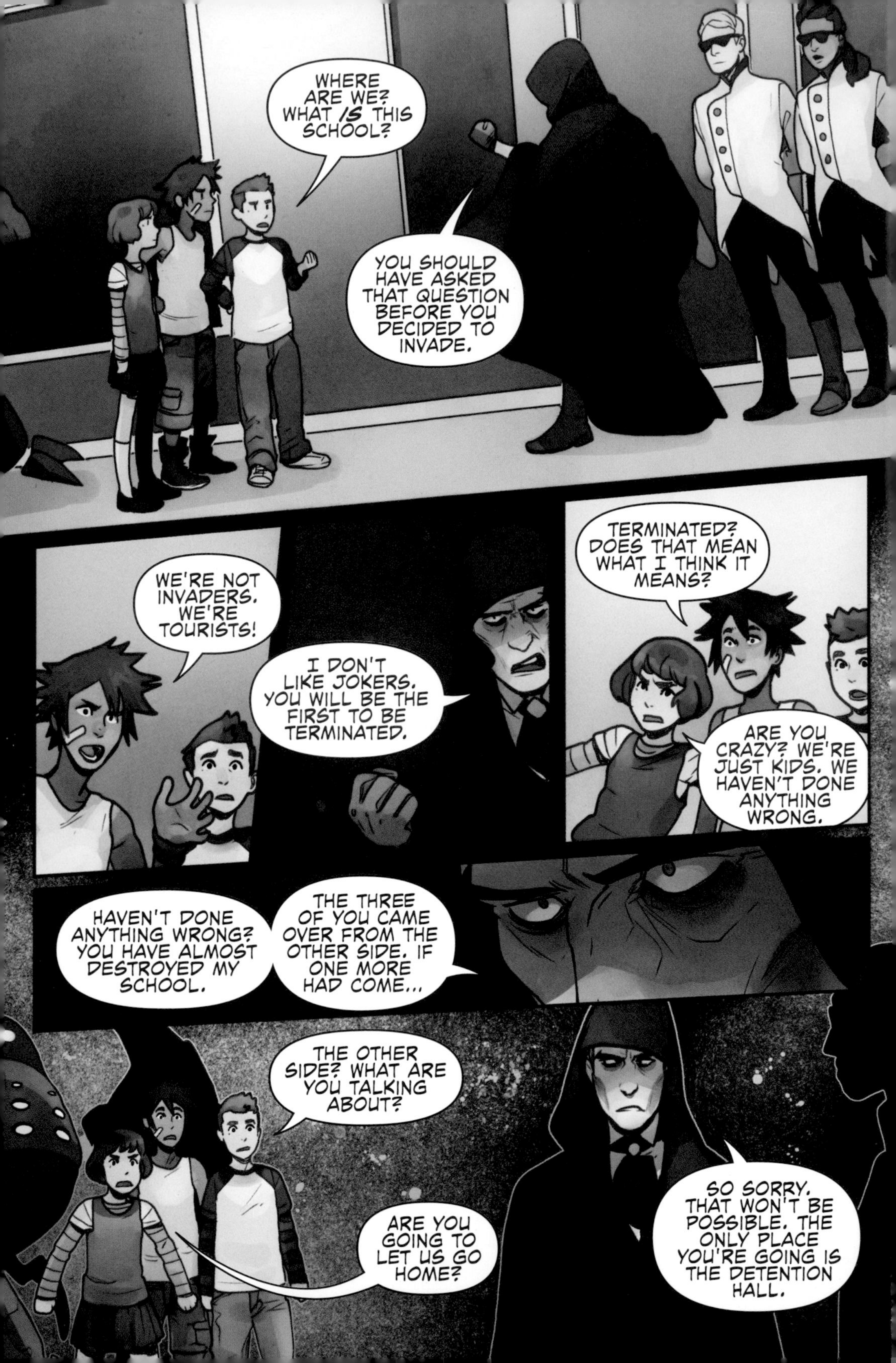
WHERE ARE WE? WHAT *IS* THIS SCHOOL?
YOU SHOULD HAVE ASKED THAT QUESTION BEFORE YOU DECIDED TO INVADE.
WE'RE NOT INVADERS. WE'RE TOURISTS!
I DON'T LIKE JOKERS. YOU WILL BE THE FIRST TO BE TERMINATED.
TERMINATED? DOES THAT MEAN WHAT I THINK IT MEANS?
ARE YOU CRAZY? WE'RE JUST KIDS. WE HAVEN'T DONE ANYTHING WRONG.
HAVEN'T DONE ANYTHING WRONG? YOU HAVE ALMOST DESTROYED MY SCHOOL.
THE THREE OF YOU CAME OVER FROM THE OTHER SIDE. IF ONE MORE HAD COME...
THE OTHER SIDE? WHAT ARE YOU TALKING ABOUT?
ARE YOU GOING TO LET US GO HOME?
SO SORRY. THAT WON'T BE POSSIBLE. THE ONLY PLACE YOU'RE GOING IS THE DETENTION HALL.

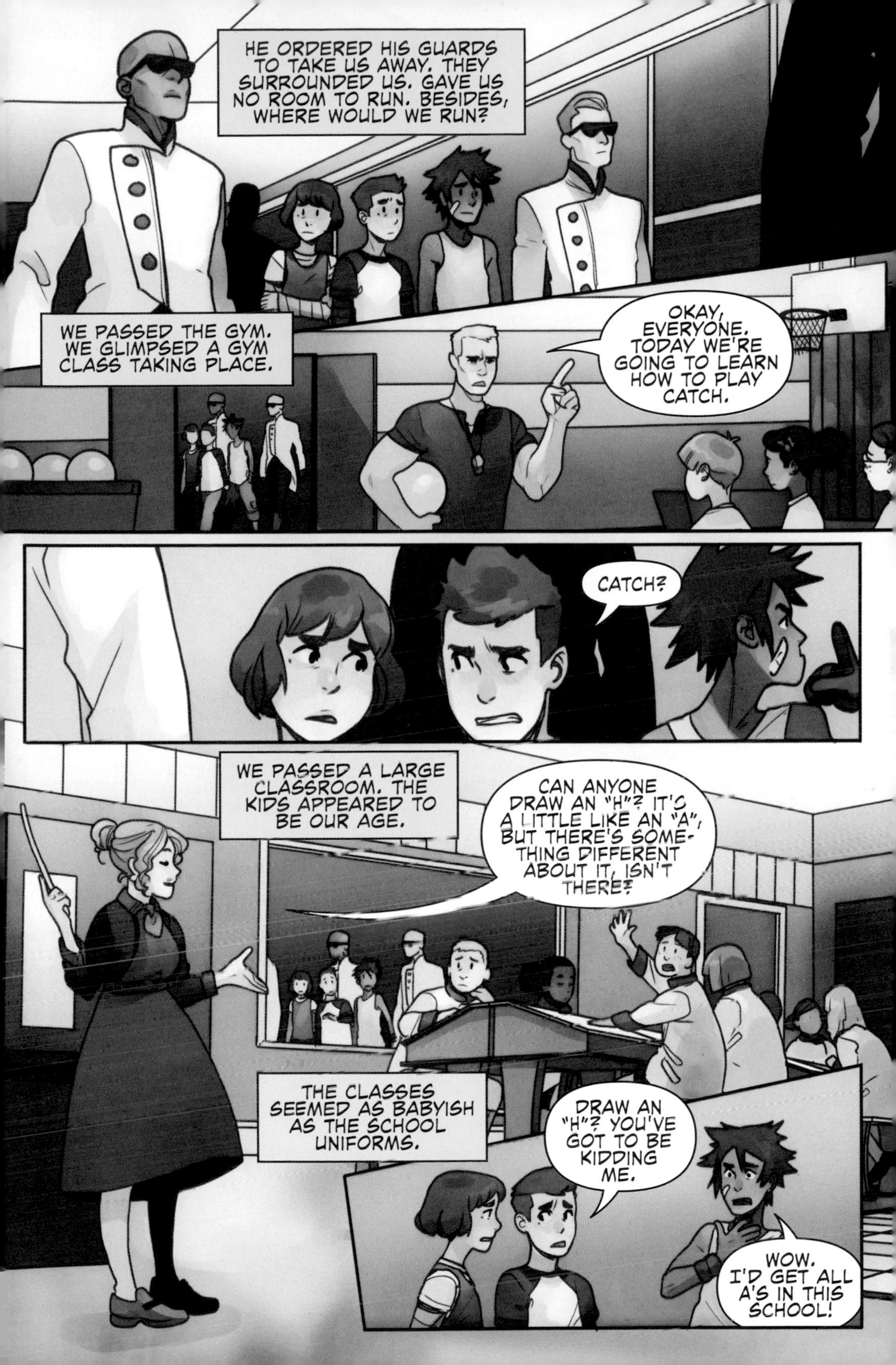

HE ORDERED HIS GUARDS TO TAKE US AWAY. THEY SURROUNDED US. GAVE US NO ROOM TO RUN. BESIDES, WHERE WOULD WE RUN?
WE PASSED THE GYM. WE GLIMPSED A GYM CLASS TAKING PLACE.
OKAY, EVERYONE. TODAY WE'RE GOING TO LEARN HOW TO PLAY CATCH.
CATCH?
WE PASSED A LARGE CLASSROOM. THE KIDS APPEARED TO BE OUR AGE.
CAN ANYONE DRAW AN "H"? IT'S A LITTLE LIKE AN "A", BUT THERE'S SOME-THING DIFFERENT ABOUT IT, ISN'T THERE?
THE CLASSES SEEMED AS BABYISH AS THE SCHOOL UNIFORMS.
DRAW AN "H"? YOU'VE GOT TO BE KIDDING ME.
WOW. I'D GET ALL A'S IN THIS SCHOOL!

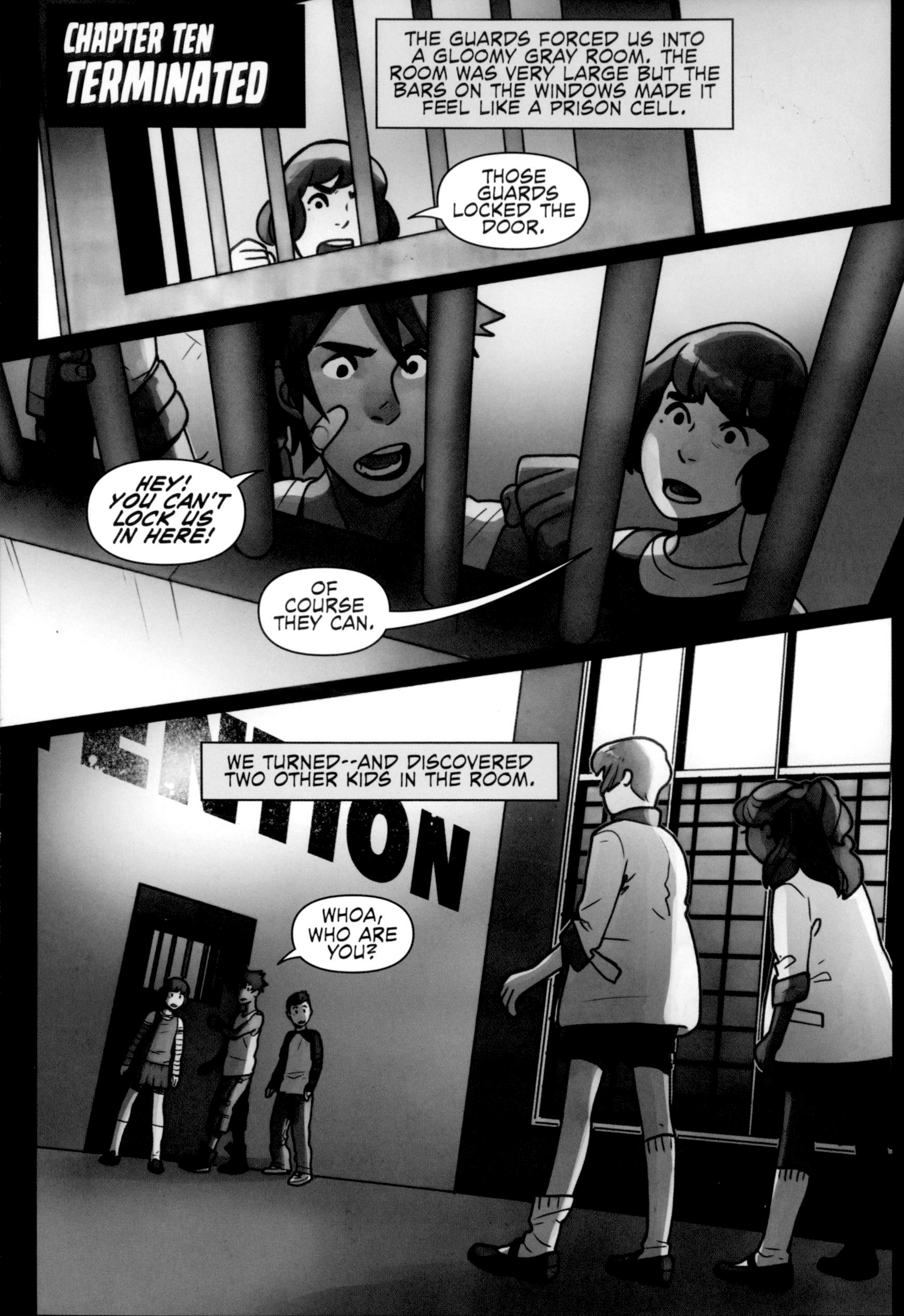
CHAPTER TEN
TERMINATED
THE GUARDS FORCED US INTO A GLOOMY GRAY ROOM. THE ROOM WAS VERY LARGE BUT THE BARS ON THE WINDOWS MADE IT FEEL LIKE A PRISON CELL.
THOSE GUARDS LOCKED THE DOOR.
HEY! YOU CAN'T LOCK US IN HERE!
OF COURSE THEY CAN.
WE TURNED--AND DISCOVERED TWO OTHER KIDS IN THE ROOM.
WHOA, WHO ARE YOU?

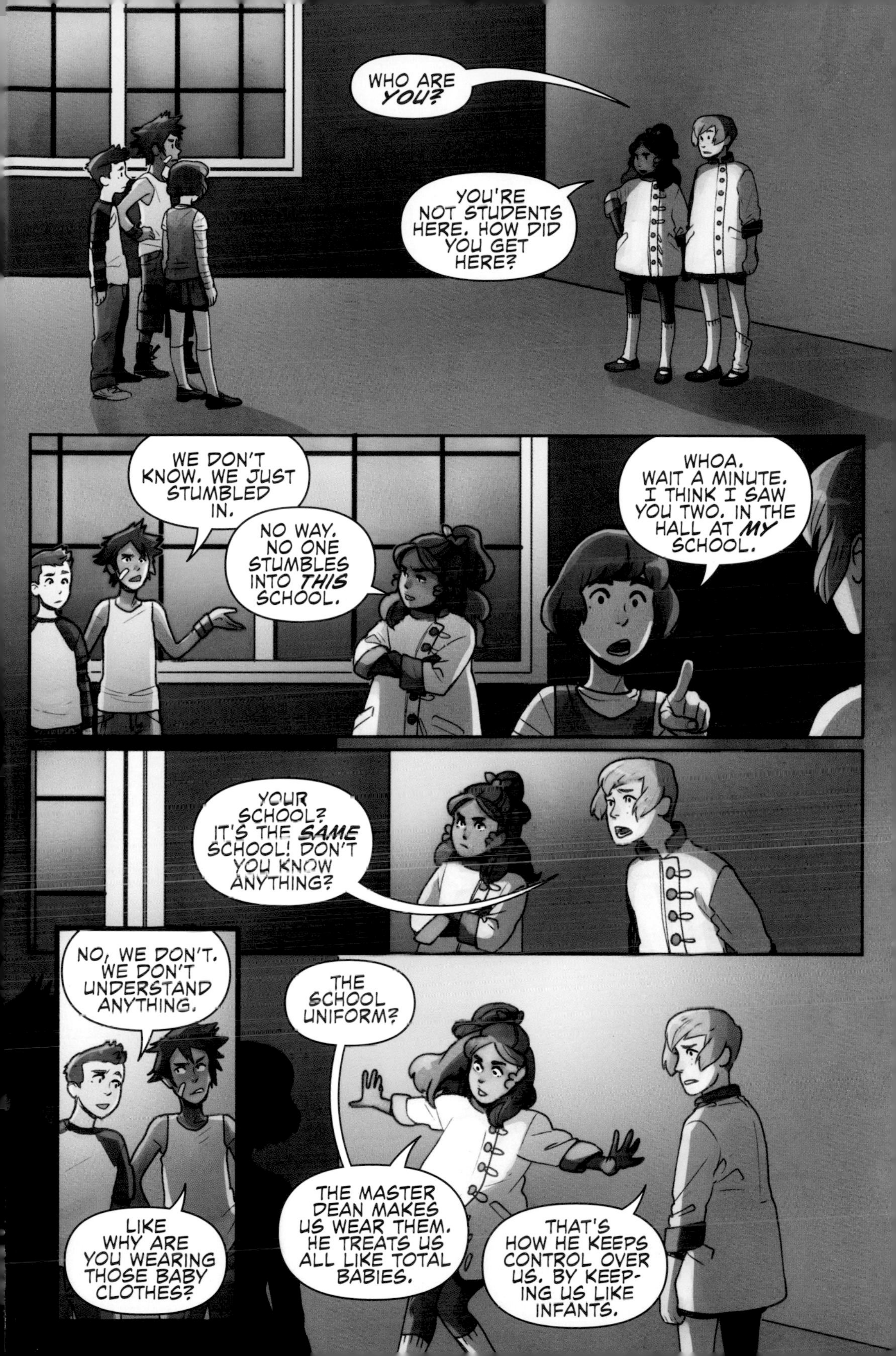
WHO ARE YOU?
YOU'RE NOT STUDENTS HERE. HOW DID YOU GET HERE?
WE DON'T KNOW. WE JUST STUMBLED IN.
NO WAY. NO ONE STUMBLES INTO THIS SCHOOL.
WHOA. WAIT A MINUTE. I THINK I SAW YOU TWO. IN THE HALL AT MY SCHOOL.
YOUR SCHOOL? IT'S THE SAME SCHOOL! DON'T YOU KNOW ANYTHING?
NO, WE DON'T. WE DON'T UNDERSTAND ANYTHING.
LIKE WHY ARE YOU WEARING THOSE BABY CLOTHES?
THE SCHOOL UNIFORM?
THE MASTER DEAN MAKES US WEAR THEM. HE TREATS US ALL LIKE TOTAL BABIES.
THAT'S HOW HE KEEPS CONTROL OVER US. BY KEEPING US LIKE INFANTS.

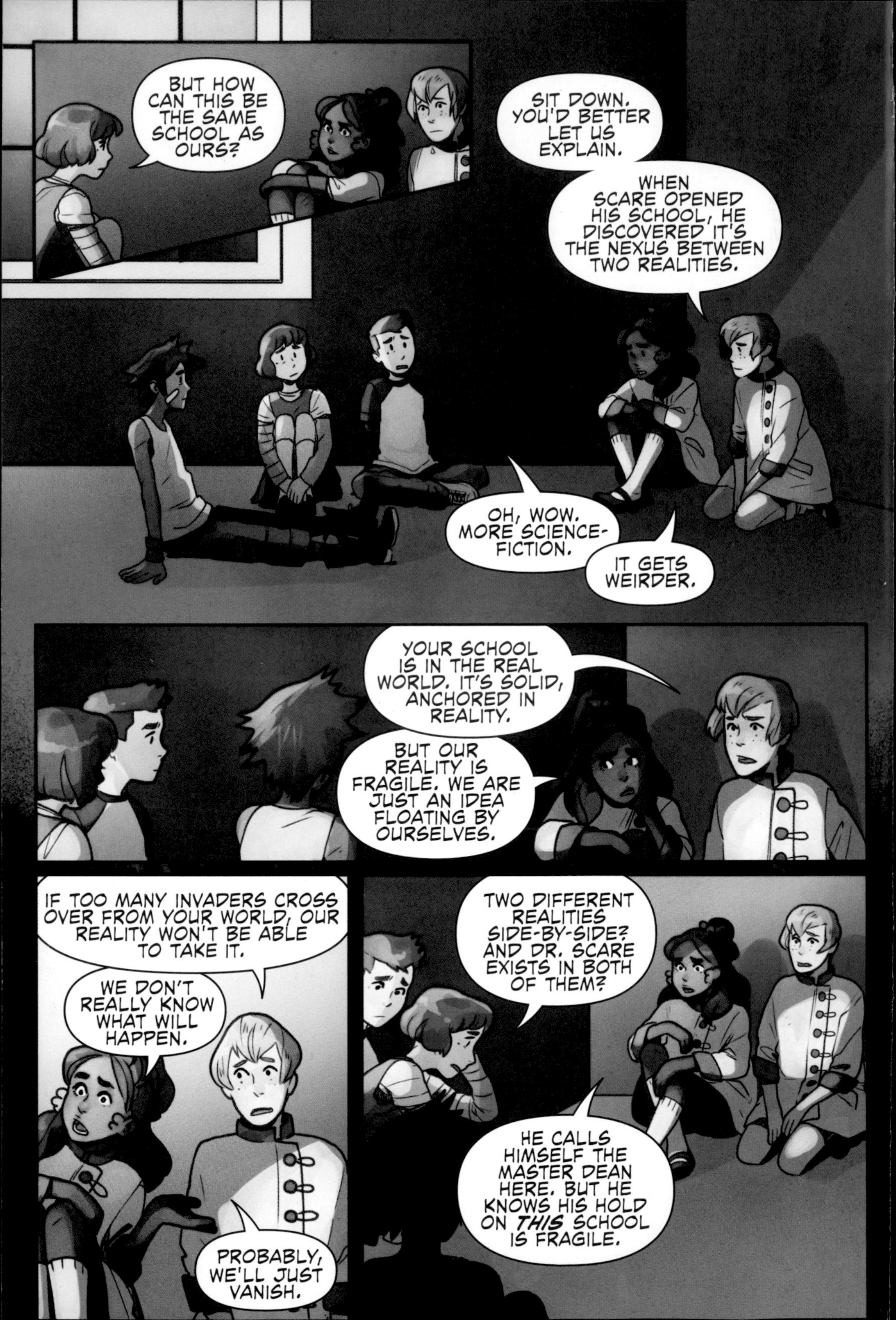
BUT HOW CAN THIS BE THE SAME SCHOOL AS OURS?
SIT DOWN. YOU'D BETTER LET US EXPLAIN.
WHEN SCARE OPENED HIS SCHOOL, HE DISCOVERED IT'S THE NEXUS BETWEEN TWO REALITIES.
OH, WOW. MORE SCIENCE-FICTION.
IT GETS WEIRDER.
YOUR SCHOOL IS IN THE REAL WORLD. IT'S SOLID, ANCHORED IN REALITY.
BUT OUR REALITY IS FRAGILE. WE ARE JUST AN IDEA FLOATING BY OURSELVES.
IF TOO MANY INVADERS CROSS OVER FROM YOUR WORLD, OUR REALITY WON'T BE ABLE TO TAKE IT.
WE DON'T REALLY KNOW WHAT WILL HAPPEN.
PROBABLY, WE'LL JUST VANISH.
TWO DIFFERENT REALITIES SIDE-BY-SIDE? AND DR. SCARE EXISTS IN BOTH OF THEM?
HE CALLS HIMSELF THE MASTER DEAN HERE. BUT HE KNOWS HIS HOLD ON THIS SCHOOL IS FRAGILE.

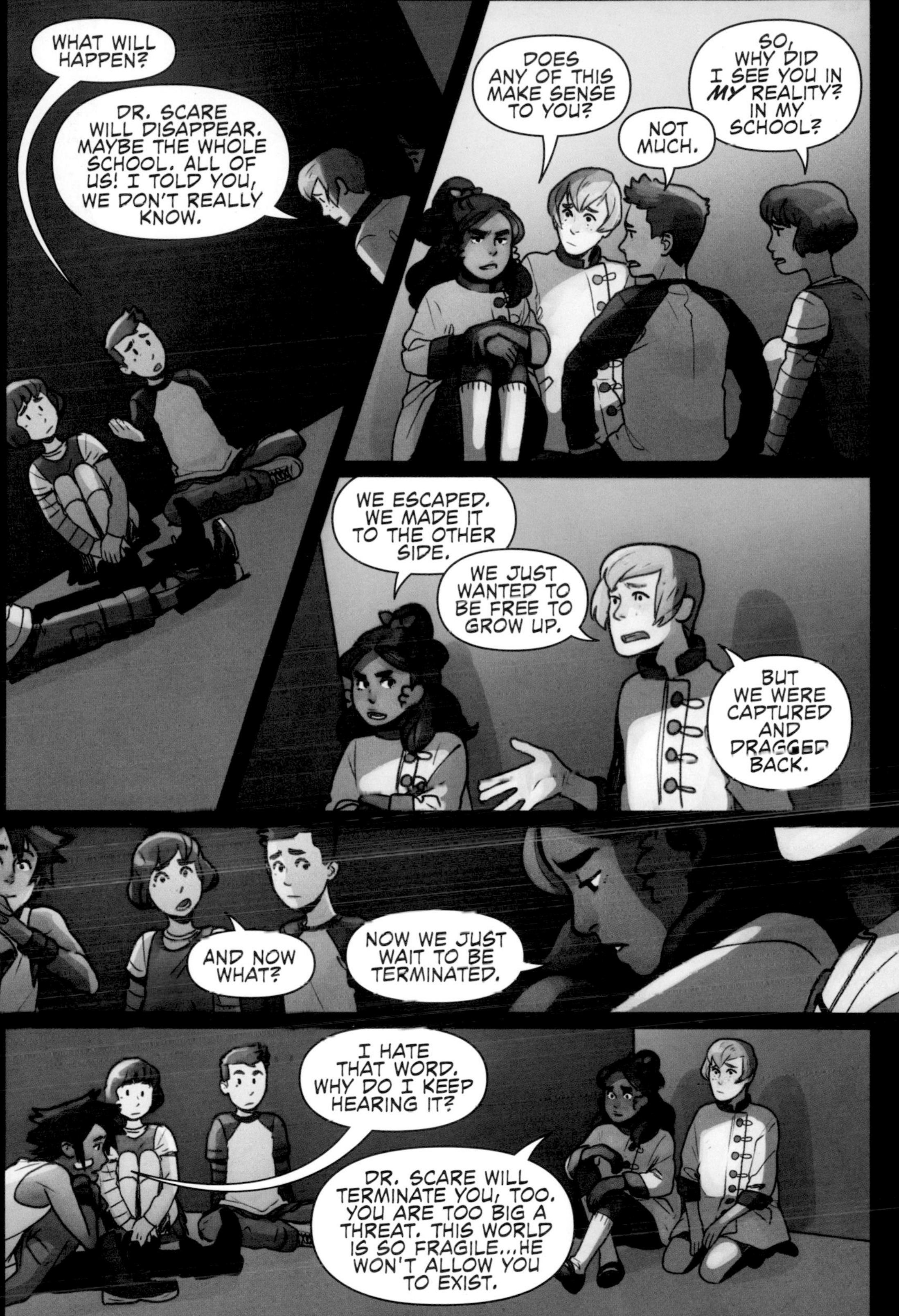
WHAT WILL HAPPEN?
DR. SCARE WILL DISAPPEAR. MAYBE THE WHOLE SCHOOL. ALL OF US! I TOLD YOU, WE DON'T REALLY KNOW.
DOES ANY OF THIS MAKE SENSE TO YOU?
NOT MUCH.
SO, WHY DID I SEE YOU IN MY REALITY? IN MY SCHOOL?
WE ESCAPED. WE MADE IT TO THE OTHER SIDE.
WE JUST WANTED TO BE FREE TO GROW UP.
BUT WE WERE CAPTURED AND DRAGGED BACK.
AND NOW WHAT?
NOW WE JUST WAIT TO BE TERMINATED.
I HATE THAT WORD. WHY DO I KEEP HEARING IT?
DR. SCARE WILL TERMINATE YOU, TOO. YOU ARE TOO BIG A THREAT. THIS WORLD IS SO FRAGILE...HE WON'T ALLOW YOU TO EXIST.

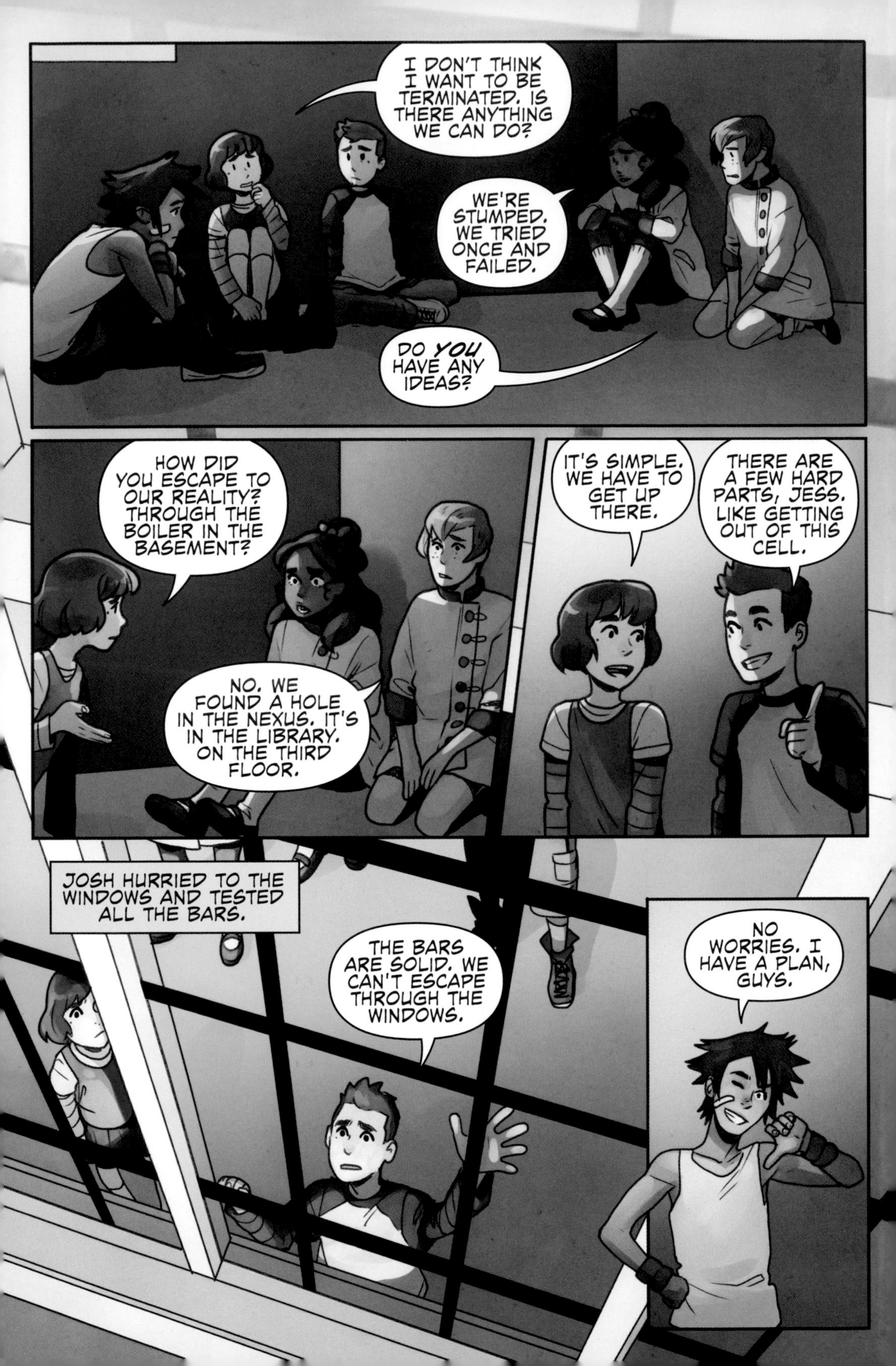
I DON'T THINK I WANT TO BE TERMINATED. IS THERE ANYTHING WE CAN DO?
WE'RE STUMPED. WE TRIED ONCE AND FAILED.
DO *YOU* HAVE ANY IDEAS?
HOW DID YOU ESCAPE TO OUR REALITY? THROUGH THE BOILER IN THE BASEMENT?
NO. WE FOUND A HOLE IN THE NEXUS. IT'S IN THE LIBRARY. ON THE THIRD FLOOR.
IT'S SIMPLE. WE HAVE TO GET UP THERE.
THERE ARE A FEW HARD PARTS, JESS. LIKE GETTING OUT OF THIS CELL.
JOSH HURRIED TO THE WINDOWS AND TESTED ALL THE BARS.
THE BARS ARE SOLID. WE CAN'T ESCAPE THROUGH THE WINDOWS.
NO WORRIES. I HAVE A PLAN, GUYS.